LAKE +
MANNING

JESSICA
HAWKINS

Editing by Elizabeth London Editing
Proofreading & Beta by Underline This Editing
Cover Design © R.B.A. Designs
Cover Photo by Perrywinkle Photography
Cover Models: Chase Williams &
Miranda McWhorter

LAKE + MANNING

ISBN: 0-9988155-4-3
ISBN-13: 978-0-9988155-4-1

TITLES BY
JESSICA HAWKINS

LEARN MORE AT JESSICAHAWKINS.NET

SLIP OF THE TONGUE
THE FIRST TASTE
YOURS TO BARE

SOMETHING IN THE WAY SERIES
SOMETHING IN THE WAY
SOMEBODY ELSE'S SKY
MOVE THE STARS
LAKE + MANNING

THE CITYSCAPE SERIES
COME UNDONE
COME ALIVE
COME TOGETHER

EXPLICITLY YOURS SERIES
POSSESSION
DOMINATION
PROVOCATION
OBSESSION

BLUEBERRY PIE

WINTER 2008

1

With oven mitts tucked under one arm and my cell balanced between my ear and shoulder, I stepped over Blue. Every winter since we'd adopted her two years ago, the dog had taken to lying in the *middle* of the kitchen whenever I baked.

"One sec," I said into the phone and bent at the hip. I flipped on the oven light and a blueberry pie appeared, crust browning right on schedule. "Perfect."

"What's perfect?" Val asked on the other end of the line.

"The pie I'm baking Manning."

"Good. They say the way to a man's heart is through his stomach."

Not exactly. After over a week away from Manning, food would be the second thing on his mind. "*They* need to think a few inches lower."

"You're such a wife, and you're not even married. I bet you're wearing an apron and everything."

"I am. It has birds on it."

"Okay, that's weird. Birds have nothing to do with cooking," Val said. "But here's what you need to do. Once Manning is full of pie and bear meat, or whatever a human his size eats, and he's half-asleep, ask him why."

"Why what?"

"The marriage thing."

I turned off the oven. I should've known she'd bring it back up, even though I'd tried to steer her off course. Diversion tactics didn't work on my best friend when she was onto something. "There's no *marriage thing*," I said, checking over my shoulder to make sure Manning hadn't snuck up on me. "Can we drop this?"

"You were telling me you weren't sure why, after four years of cohabitation—"

"One of which I commuted to Los Angeles for work," I said, "and three of which I've lived part-time in Pomona."

She ignored me. "You were saying you don't know why Manning hasn't proposed yet."

"That's not what I said." With a sigh, I removed the pie from the oven and set it on a burner. "I already know why he hasn't—I told him not to until I was done with school."

"You said you didn't want to get *married* until you were done with school—and you're graduating next summer. He can still propose."

I hated to admit Val had a point. What I'd actually started to explain before I'd remembered Val would take *anything* juicy and run with it, was how Manning used to bug me constantly about getting married . . . but lately, he'd been uncharacteristically quiet on the topic. Between his furniture business and me being gone four days a week for school, marriage had hardly come up at all the last six or so months. I wasn't wondering why he hadn't proposed—I wanted to know why he'd given up *trying* to propose.

Because Manning had ways of getting what he wanted. We'd once spent three weeks arguing over whether I needed snow tread tires for my car. Snow in Big Bear was pretty mild, and when it wasn't, we took Manning's truck. Winter tires were expensive.

I'd given in out of exhaustion.

Manning wanted to get married, of that I was certain. He would've sealed the deal the warm September day I'd moved in except that I'd made him promise to wait. That, and he wanted the wedding to be special, and right now, neither of us had time for anything more than a quick trip to City Hall. Manning's business kept him busy around the clock. I went to school two hours away, so I'd rented an apartment where I stayed during the week. Our life had not yet *begun*.

But it would soon. I had one semester left of classes before graduating in May, and surely that had crossed Manning's mind. "I'm not going to dope him up on blueberry pie and ask him to ask me to marry him. Especially since I don't even know if I want that yet."

"You won't *let* yourself want it because you've been burned in the past."

"Not true. I want it eventually, but with our schedules—"

"Blah, blah, blah. Listen, if the pie doesn't get him to drop to one knee, withhold sex until he caves. I assume you're naked under your apron."

I laughed. "I am not. And I don't need Manning to cave. He and I have no secrets. If I'm ready for a proposal, I can just tell him."

"Where's the fun in that?" she asked. "In my plan, you get pie *and* sex."

"I'm already getting those things. Since I was gone all last week for exams, I'm surprising him with a home-cooked meal and . . . other things." I didn't need an excuse to feed us both into a coma or climb Manning·like the mountain of a man he was. Nor did I need one to broach the subject of marriage—should I decide to do such a thing.

"He thinks you're still in Pomona?" she asked.

"Until tomorrow." Blue raised her head to look at me with her signature turquoise eyes. I put my index finger over my lips. "Don't tell Daddy."

"Ew," Val said. "You call him Daddy?"

"I was talking to Blue." I squatted to scratch her stomach. Manning and I had decided to foster pets until after graduation when I'd be living at home full-time. Blue was a Border Collie-Australian Shepherd mix—or so we guessed—named after the striking color of her eyes. She'd been the third dog we'd taken in. I'd cried buckets when the shelter had placed the second dog, so Manning had suggested we keep Blue. He'd said it was to prevent more tears, but it was no secret Manning had a weakness for blue eyes.

When the front door opened, Blue perked up. "He's here," I whispered to Val. "I'll call you later."

"Tell him to put a ring on it," she cried.

"I don't even want to know how many times you've listened to Beyoncé's new album," I said before I hung up.

"Lake?" Manning called, stomping through the foyer.

I stood and smoothed out my apron before quickly scrubbing flour from my wrist. "In the kitchen."

He came in wiping his temple on his sleeve. "You said you were driving in tomorrow morning."

I had about two seconds to get a good look at him—flannel open at the collar, a week's worth of beard, and hair pushed off his face—before he had me off my feet and wrapped in one of his strong bear hugs.

"I decided to surprise you," I said.

"I hate surprises." He inhaled my hair. "There's ice on the roads and it's dark out. If anything had happened—"

"Want me to come back tomorrow?"

He growled into my neck and set me on the counter. "A week's too long, Lake."

I let my head fall back as he trailed kisses up my throat. He pulled me to the edge, urging my legs around him. "*Manning*," I said when his tool belt pressed my inner thighs. "Your drill."

"That's not my drill, Birdy." He snickered as he unhooked his belt and let it hit the ground with a *thunk* that made me jump.

"Watch out for Blue!"

"She knows to get out of the way when Mama Bear comes home."

I laughed as he tickled the underside of my jaw with his overgrown stubble. "Why are you still wearing all that anyway?" I asked.

"Huh?" he said, leaning in for a kiss.

I pulled back. "Usually you leave your belt in the workshop at the end of the day."

"I was coming in to grab a bite."

I pushed my palms into his chest, using all my strength to keep him from devouring me. "A bite?" I asked. "What about those frozen meals I left you?"

"That's a bite for me. I was going to put one in the microwave—"

"You mean oven."

"Right."

"Then what?"

"Down the hatch and back to work. Can we talk about this after?"

I arched an eyebrow. I'd expected enthusiasm from him, naturally, but Manning was coming at me like *I* was blueberry pie. "After *what*?"

He sighed, relenting enough to let me push him back. "I missed you. You can't expect me not to be eager."

"Phone sex not cutting it?" I joked.

He leveled me with a glare. "You know it doesn't. I'm just happy to have you to myself for more than a weekend."

"Thank heavens for Christmas break." I played with one of his shirt buttons while keeping my distance. "But it's after seven. Why were you going back out there?"

"What do you think I do when you're not here?" He licked his lips as he stared at mine. "I work."

"Not tonight, you don't."

He squeezed my hips, bringing me against his crotch. "I never work late when you're here. That was our deal. No matter what's going on, if we're both in town, we always eat dinner together."

I kissed his forehead and slid off the counter despite his grunted protest. "First, we eat."

"But it's been almost two weeks."

"It's been eight days." I picked up his tool belt and set it on the counter. "There's lasagna in the oven, and I'm cooling a pie for dessert."

As I'd predicted, that silenced him. Food was the one thing that had the potential to hold over Manning's sex drive, at least for a bit.

"You were supposed to have dinner with classmates tonight to celebrate getting exams out of the way."

"There was no dinner." Bent over to check on the lasagna, I looked back at him and grinned. "I lied."

"*Lied?*" He hooked a finger in my apron string and tugged me backward. "To me? Who do you think you're dealing with here?"

I pushed his hand away and shuffled back to the oven. "Hand me the mitts."

He put them on himself and pulled the dish out to set it next to the pie. "Nothing like your homemade meals," he said. "My mouth is watering."

"Patience. I won't be responsible for yet *another* of your burnt tongues. Why don't you go shut down the shop?" I asked, turning to get a spatula.

He took my elbow, pulling me back until I was against his chest. "Thank you," he said.

Tucked into him, I let out a long breath. As much as I liked to tease Manning for his grumpiness when we were apart, I felt our distance, too. Every hour of every day. There were times I was tempted to drop out and leave Pomona so we could finally start our lives together, but it was the closest college to us with a veterinary program. "What're you thanking me for?" I asked. "I haven't done anything yet."

Blue tried to nose between us. Manning scratched behind her ear while keeping me close. "You're home early. That's worth giving thanks for."

"I wish I could be here more."

"I want that, too, you know I do, but it's not forever."

Even though I knew our distance bothered Manning, he'd been nothing but supportive of my career. He'd stuck by me as I'd finished out my contract in Hollywood, *then* when I'd turned around and picked a university that was also two hours away. Over the last decade and a half, we'd gotten pretty used to being apart. Maybe what we needed now was a piece—or even a promise—of forever.

Damn it, Val. It was possible she'd known exactly what seed she was planting when she'd brought up marriage. That girl had always been wiser than she looked.

And then, any thoughts in my head vanished. Manning bent down and shook the ground I stood on with a slow, sweet kiss. "Should've done that as soon as I walked in the door," he said.

"You were excited," I teased, sliding my arms around his neck.

"Still am." He thumbed the corner of my mouth. "Your lips are all red. If I'd known you were coming tonight, I would've shaved."

I ran the back of my hand over the short beard he'd grown during the week we'd been apart. "You never let it get this long."

"Because I don't like to scratch you up."

"So if I weren't around, you'd go full Sasquatch?"

"Nah. All this hair itches. I'm just too lazy to shave it when you're gone."

Considering it was December, I kind of dug the mountain man look, but if he didn't want to shave, I'd do it for him. He did enough for me on a daily basis; tonight was about him.

"Dinner's almost ready," I said, slipping out of his arms. "Go lock up. I have plans for you later."

"Plans?" He patted my behind and picked up his belt from the counter on his way out the door. "Can't wait."

I turned back to Blue, who looked from me to the food as if I might *finally* break down and scoop a serving into her dog dish. A home-cooked meal, blueberry pie, and sex—that was a plan, wasn't it? A good one, too. No sense in bringing up anything as serious as marriage tonight.

If only I could stop thinking about it.

2

While Manning did the dishes, I laid a towel over the counter in our master bath, filled a cup under the faucet, and got his razor from a cabinet.

Manning came in rubbing his stomach. "I think I ate too much."

"I told you not to have that second piece of pie."

He nodded at the scene unfolding in front him. "What's all this?"

"Get a chair from the dining room."

"You gonna shave me?"

"You said you needed one." I glanced at him over my shoulder. "And you're always raving about how much you love—"

"Shaving *you*? Mmm." He came up behind me, catching my eye in the mirror above our sinks as he slid a hand down my tummy. "Speaking of, you should be due for one yourself."

I relaxed against his front as he pushed his hand into the waist of my jeans. "Some of my friends at school have started waxing," I told him as he toyed with the lace band of my thong. "Do you want me to do that? It's cleaner."

"And put me out of the job?" he rasped into my ear, his wandering fingers making my breath catch. "You know how much I love to do it."

Manning was a true creative. It was something everyone else overlooked. He hadn't *just* built our home. He didn't *just* put furniture together. He designed with attention to every detail. And he'd designed me, too. We'd spent many nights in the clawfoot tub he'd chosen and installed. He shaved my legs, took his time on my bikini line so he wouldn't nick me, and was never satisfied until it was exactly as he wanted it. It always led to sex. His focus and care, and the slow, controlled way he groomed me until he was content, was a special kind of foreplay.

Tempted to give in to him, I blinked away my haze and forced myself back to reality. I'd get mine soon enough, but first I wanted to pamper this man who worked way too hard. I urged his hand from my pants. "Later," I said. "Right now, what I really need is a chair."

"Coming right up."

Once he'd left, I checked that I had everything I needed. Or at least what I'd seen Manning use in the mornings. He returned with a dining chair and sat facing the mirror. Behind him, I clipped a hand towel around his shoulders then tilted his chin back until he was looking upside down at me. "This is my first time," I said. "How do I do it?"

"I don't know. Just shave."

"Do I go with or against the grain?"

"I go against but I never really thought about it."

I went to stand in front of him. "You do this almost every day. It never occurred to you to make sure to do it right?"

"The hair's gone each morning, isn't it?"

With a sigh, I shook my head and filled my palm with shaving cream. I smoothed it over his jaw, careful not to get it in his hairline—or up his nose as I covered his upper lip.

"You're being way too nice about this whole thing," he said. "Slap on the cream and slice away."

"Sit there a few minutes and let the cream soften the hair," I said, ignoring him. "I'm going to look up how to do this properly."

"It's not a big deal."

"No? Is that how you shave me—slice away?"

He frowned. "Of course not."

"Then let me do this my way." I stuck out my tongue and went to our shared office, which had only a desk with a chair, a printer, and some lightweight file cabinets. It was the smallest room in the house and closest to the master—perfect for a nursery—but Manning had set up there temporarily because it let the most light in. I sat at the computer, ran a search on how to shave a man's face, and returned to the bathroom with one of the articles.

Manning slow-blinked at me. "You printed out *directions?*"

"I want to do it right. Step one," I read, "apply cream and let the hair soften." I gave Manning a *told-you-so* look in the mirror and scanned the rest of the instructions before swapping them for his razor. "You don't take care of yourself when I'm gone."

"Where's that coming from?"

I stood between his knees, tilted his chin up, and slid the razor down his jaw. "You don't shave correctly. You're supposed to go *with* the grain."

"I'm a grown man, Lake."

"Are you? When I'm not here, you don't eat enough vegetables. You smoke more."

"Nah."

"Don't pretend you don't. Also, you work from dawn 'til dusk. Maybe it's time to put an ad in the paper. If you had help around here, you could cut back. And you'd see a real human each day so you'd have to look presentable." I pulled back to inspect my progress on his right cheek. "I worry you're lonely up here all by yourself."

"I am," he said, running a hand up the outside of my thigh. "That's no secret."

"Even after I graduate, I'll be working long hours. I can't be here all the time."

"Lake, I don't need anything other than what we've got. I'm not looking to make more friends or hire someone who'll be in my business."

"They'll be in your *shed*, working side by side with you. It doesn't mean you have to give up any control."

"I do have to give up money, though. I suspect this person'll want to get paid."

"The whole idea is that they produce more, and you make more."

"Doubt that when I'd have to double check their work all day long."

"That's called *trust*. And letting go. And delegation." I frowned at his purposeful stubbornness. "I know you don't need a business lesson. I just want you to go easier on yourself."

His eyes roamed over my face. "You should take your own advice."

"I can't." I tilted his chin back even farther to get to his neck. "In my case, sometimes, we're talking life or death. I have to be as prepared as possible before I start working with people's pets."

"See? We're each getting established still. It'll come. Give it time."

I set down the razor and toweled off the remaining shaving cream. He shut his eyes as I wiped his jaw, then while I raked my fingers through the sides of his hair. If I was going to bring up marriage, this was about as good an opening as I could ask for. My palms got suddenly clammy. He looked so relaxed, probably for the first time since I'd left—and did I really *need* to pester him about why he'd suddenly dropped the subject? Manning was a deliberate man. Whatever they were, he had his reasons.

"Feels good," he murmured. "I need you, Lake." He pulled me between his legs by my hips, his eyes trailing up my stomach and over my breasts in a way that tightened my insides. "I have since you walked in the door."

"Not yet," I said.

"Now." He stood and swooped me up before I could protest, carrying me toward the bedroom.

"I have one more thing planned," I said, pushing his chest. "Reroute to the den."

"Mmm, yeah," he said, pivoting and heading the opposite direction down the hall. "We haven't done it in there in a while."

I rolled my eyes as he stopped short in the doorway of the den. "When did you do all this?"

"While you were working. Put me down and get the fireplace going."

Once on the ground, I set to work lighting the candles on the mantel I'd put out before dinner. In the middle of the room, near the fireplace on a sheepskin rug, I'd made a bed of pillows.

Manning looked back at me while stocking the fireplace. "Johnnie Walker Blue Label?" he asked as I poured us drinks at a side table. "What's the occasion?"

"You." I set his tumbler aside. "I know you weren't happy I wanted to stay in Pomona and study last week. And I'm sure you worked yourself to the bone. I'm giving you a long massage to make up for it."

He lit a roll of newspaper and held it up the chimney to warm the flue. "You think you're strong enough to take on these knots?"

"Oh, yes." I grinned, picking up massage oil and flexing my bicep. "Nobody knows your body like I do, Great Bear. I'm going to hit all your sweet spots."

He actually shuddered.

I perched on the edge of the couch and motioned for him to sit on the floor between my legs. "Strip."

He elbowed off his flannel, tossing it aside as he got to the ground. I squirted oil on his shoulders and rubbed it over his upper back and biceps. Massaging him was like kneading concrete and after a few minutes, with the fire in full effect, my hairline started to perspire. I readjusted on the couch, my thigh muscles aching from holding my legs open.

"Doing all right?" he asked.

"Yep." I worked the back of his neck, running my fingers up to his scalp then down his spine. The California sun was strong, even in winter, and despite his naturally bronzed skin, he had a faint tan line at the back of his neck. "Is it making any difference?"

"Yeah, Birdy." He laughed. "But you're sweating on me."

I pinched his arm. "You love it."

He looked over his shoulder and up at me. "Come here."

I leaned over his front, sliding my hands down his pecs from behind, flipping my long hair over his shoulder to nuzzle his neck. He pulled me closer by my arms. "*There's* the sweet spot," he said as I massaged his abs of stone, my fingers inching lower and lower.

He released my arm to pick up his whisky from the side table, took a sip, and passed it back to me. The burn of liquor, of the fireplace on my skin, loosened my limbs.

"You're shaking." He trapped my knees with his biceps, pulling my legs to his sides and massaging my calves.

"Your shoulders are too wide." I put the glass next to him on the ground. "My thighs hurt."

He scooted forward, away from me. "I've never heard a better invitation. I'm more than happy to relieve your aching thighs."

"Tonight's about you. Get on the rug so I can work on *yours*."

"When did you get so bossy?" he asked but went to lie on the floor where I'd piled the pillows. He stuffed one under his chest, resting his chin on his forearms. "Persistent? Impulsive? Yes. But my little bird used to have a shy side."

"You've spent the last few years touching, licking, and kissing the shy right out of me," I pointed out, sitting on his ass.

"I have, haven't I?" he asked, a smile in his voice. "How come Blue's not nudging her snout up my ass?"

"I put her out back."

"You really planned this out."

"Shh." I ran my thumbs up the muscles around his spine. "Try to relax."

Once I'd located a knot, I used one elbow, then both, to get deeper. I added more and more pressure until he groaned. "All right, you win," he said. "That feels fucking great."

When I hit a sore spot, he bucked his hips. As turned on as I was easing the aches in my strong man, as much as I wanted him to pull me into his arms and make love to me, I mostly wished he'd be able to relax until I'd exhausted myself.

Of course, I had no delusions that would actually happen. There'd be no end to the massage or start to sex. Manning's groans deepened as I hit his lower back. I dipped my fingers under the waistband of his jeans, kneading the top of his ass.

"Don't neglect the front," he said.

I slickened my palms with more oil. He lifted his hips as I slid my hands down the front of his pants and stroked him once, long and slow. I sat back as he flipped over and took his pants off. There'd be no more subduing the bear, so I gave in and climbed on.

"Your face is pink," he said.

"I'm warm from the fire."

He opened my blouse, offering slight relief from the heat. I shut my eyes as he slid my top off my shoulders, then unbuttoned my jeans. "Let me see you," he said.

He could already see as much of me as he wanted, but as always, he wanted my eyes open. I looked down at him, leaning my hands on his chest. My hair made a curtain around us, his abs tensing as the ends grazed his skin. "Even lit up by the fire," he said, shoving a hand in the front of my jeans, "you look angelic."

I sucked in a breath as he circled his fingertips over my clit through my underwear. "Maybe it's a disguise to lure you in," I said, biting my lip.

"It's working." He slipped aside the crotch of my panties. "The question is, how deep do you want me?"

I bent forward to hover my mouth above his. "Do you have a setting other than 'as deep as possible'?" I asked.

He fought against my jeans to push two fingers inside me, flicking them until my thighs shook for a different reason. With the tight fit, his palm massaged my clit. "Are you teasing me?" he asked, withdrawing his hand. "Because that's a two-way street."

"I doubt that's a game you want to play." Worked up from the massage, I was nearly panting already. I wiggled off his lap to kiss my way over his pecs and abs, letting my hair trail on his skin, knowing how it tickled and aroused him. Pulling down his underwear, I licked the underside of his shaft while raking my nails along his inner thighs. As I tongued the tip of his cock, I glanced at him from under my lashes.

By the time he gave in and fisted the hair at my scalp, he was writhing beneath me. "You win," he said. "Put your mouth on me."

"Not yet." I smirked. Once, turning Manning on had been an adventure, his body new territory to chart. Now, I could follow the map with my eyes closed and had many times. Just as he knew a feathered touch along my ribs always made my breath hitch, I knew grazing a fingernail under his balls turned his erection from stone to pure steel. Gone were the days of my timidity and uncertainty. When I took Manning in my mouth, I did it with the confidence that I could send him to heaven with a blowjob—and also that he wouldn't let me. When he was as turned on as he was now, he never finished anywhere but balls deep inside me.

I sucked Manning with everything I had, to make him feel like a king, to show him how I worshipped him—and I didn't stop until he started to come apart beneath me. I had him partway down my throat when he tugged me up by my hair.

I stood to peel off my jeans, taking my time so he could watch. I didn't have to ask how he wanted me. Whenever we fucked after time apart, he had to be able to touch me everywhere, look me in the eye, watch my face as I climaxed. That first time, he wanted me raw so he could come inside me. After he'd had his fill, he might fuck me from behind or ask me to swallow him, but never that first time.

I slipped my underwear down to my ankles and stepped out of them to stand over him.

"Are you wet enough or you want me to eat you out first?" he asked.

With only his words and the flicker of his tongue over his bottom lip, my knees weakened. "I don't think I can wait," I said.

"Me neither."

As I lowered myself, he took my hips, positioning them over him. I braced my hands against his chest and sank onto him. Some nights, he couldn't get inside me fast enough. Others, he allowed me to take control, to tease both of us as I let myself adjust to his size. It didn't matter how many times we'd been together, our union always felt like the first time— overwhelming, big, thick.

Manning squeezed my waist until his fingertips nearly touched. He cupped my breasts as I rocked on him, thumbing my nipples, then wrapping his hands loosely around my neck. He held me in place as he took over, thrusting up into me so I could do nothing but take all of him and moan each time he hit the right spot.

He flipped me onto my back. The right side of my body cooled quickly away from the fire. His first thrust from on top came undiluted, hard and deep, the manifestation of his ache to be inside me all day.

He dropped his forehead to mine, and without warning, he slowed, lengthening his thrusts, as if stroking his cock with me. He kissed me with the same gentle control, both of us appreciating the simple joy of being there together.

"Let's make love here every night," he murmured.

"Life is not that good," I said. "It can't be."

"It can. It is."

My heart swelled, and I held on more tightly as he picked up his pace. One of his hands roamed down my side and over my hip, pulling my thigh up until my knee was bent. He reached underneath me, teasing forbidden spots that he knew put me on the brink of climax. I let myself get lost in him, in the desperate and loving way he took me, and when he was ready to come, he made sure I did first.

As my orgasm worked through me, he moved my hands above my head. I barely felt the grip of his fingers laced with mine, the grunts that rumbled his chest, and then the hot, slick way he filled me.

Manning rolled onto his back, sweating with labored breaths. I stayed where I was, boneless and sinking into the pillows. After a few moments, he squeezed an arm underneath me to pull me into his side. "I thought I was eating frozen leftovers by myself and jerking off tonight," he said, eyes already closed. "I can hardly believe my luck."

23

He murmured his last words, fading fast. I was still wide awake. "You jerk off when I'm not here?" I teased.

"Hmm."

"To what?" I shifted up to rest my arm on his chest and my chin on the back of my hand so I could see him. "Internet porn?"

A grunt was his only response. I'd lost him. I took a few moments to study his serene face. I'd accomplished what I'd wanted—I'd spoiled him into a coma. But alone with my thoughts, Val's questions floated to the front of my mind. How long until I got to call myself his wife? I'd waited years to be his at all. Even though I was the one who'd wanted to put off marriage, it didn't really make sense to me anymore. Once I graduated and moved back in fulltime, there was no reason not to have a wedding.

Manning's breathing had evened out. Now probably wasn't the right time to bring up marriage.

Then again, when had either of us ever gotten our timing right?

3

The crackling fire warmed Manning's dark features as he dozed. Flames made shadows on his strong, angular face, his expression still and peaceful because of our lovemaking. It wasn't helping my sudden impatience to bring up marriage that he looked handsome as ever.

"Are you awake?" I asked.

"Mmm."

"You know I love our life."

It took a couple seconds, but just like I knew it would, that brought Manning back to consciousness. He opened one eye. "What?"

I traced a circle in his chest hair. "And in the past, I said I wanted to finish school before we made any big changes."

"And *I* said we've already waited long enough."

"Exactly."

"Exactly what?" He scanned my face. "Hard as I try, I can't read your mind. You want to ask me something, do it."

Manning always reminded me he couldn't read my mind, but I didn't believe that for a moment. He knew what I wanted—he always seemed to, anyway. It was the small things, like when he brought me tea some nights while I studied, and others, he seemed to sense when I'd hit a wall. He'd carry me off to bed, even when I protested that I should push through a few more hours. I didn't have to ask for what I wanted very often, and since there was no bigger request than "marry me," it made me shy. "You really don't know?" I asked.

"Yeah." He tucked some of my hair behind my ear. "But I need you to say it."

I blew out a breath. "Remember a few months ago, we were on that hike in the woods, and you stopped to tie your shoes?"

He laughed a little. "We've been on a lot of hikes, Lake."

"But you got down on one knee, and I wasn't expecting anything, but the way you did it, it looked like . . . I mean, I know it's dumb, but . . . ." Like it had in that moment, my heart skipped with the possibility of Manning proposing. "I'm embarrassed to admit where my mind went. And not for the first time."

"You told me not to propose."

"Since when do you listen to me?"

The dimple that appeared when he half-smiled made me want to forget this whole thing and ravage him again. "For once," he said with amusement, "I'm not the one bringing this up."

"You used to all the time, but you don't anymore." I lowered my eyes to his chest. "I know you're not having second thoughts about us, but . . . are you having second thoughts?"

He laughed. "No, Birdy. Of course not. It's because other things have been taking up space in my mind."

Other things? What other things? Manning had a terribly sweet habit of putting me first *all the time*. He'd once canceled his workday to drive me into Pomona when my car had broken down the morning of an exam—one reason I'd started staying at school before anything important. Then he'd picked me up at the end of that week in my newly fixed car. Any night I was home to make dinner, he stopped everything the moment I called for him, even when he was in the zone. In the bedroom, my needs came first—literally. If he was thinking about something other than me or work, I couldn't say I blamed him— but it was out of character. "What things?"

He looked up at the ceiling, blinking a few times as if choosing his words. "I like to think one of the lessons I've learned over the years is that *perfect* doesn't exist. The day I marry you, finally hearing you're my wife will be enough, but I can't help that I want it to be as close to perfect as possible."

My nerves fizzled out. I thought we'd moved on from this. At first, Manning had stayed away because he was afraid he'd ruin me. Then, it'd taken him years to bring me to the home he'd built us due to some ridiculous expectations he'd invented. I hadn't needed perfection then, and I didn't now. I just needed Manning. I couldn't help feeling as if this was a setback for us. "I don't need some grand-gesture proposal, Manning. Ask whenever you're ready. Then, we can go to City Hall for all I care."

The way he scolded me with a simple look, I could see City Hall was not an option.

"I don't need or even want perfect," I continued. "Especially if it means you're going to put distance between us the way you have in the past."

His expression eased. "Let me rephrase. I don't need perfect. All I care about, and I think you want this, too, is that the wedding is *us*. And we are far from perfect."

"Exactly," I said. "So what's the problem?"

"I never want you to look back at that day with any regrets."

"Are you kidding? How could you think . . ." *Regret.* The meaning of his words dawned on me. When Manning spoke of regret, it was usually in regard to one thing. "Is this about my family?"

He scratched the bridge of his nose and said, "They should be there."

"We've been over this. They don't want to be there, and I've made my peace with that."

"So you've talked with them about this?" he asked.

He knew I hadn't. I spoke to my mom and Tiffany even less frequently than I had when I'd lived in New York. I couldn't just come out and tell them I was with Manning. Not only did the idea of it make my stomach churn, but it wasn't news to break over the phone. On the rare occasion we did talk, keeping them in the dark about the most important part of my life felt like lying. It was easier not speaking to them at all.

Not bothering to hold back a scowl, I started to get up. "I haven't, but I guess you have."

Manning tugged me back onto his chest by my elbow. "Your dad and I mainly talk about my business. He has no idea I speak to you, as you know." He sighed. "My point is that you don't know what they want. You're using that as an excuse not to make the first move."

"Are you giving me an ultimatum?" I asked. "If I don't make up with my family, you won't marry me?"

"Come on now. You *know* there's nothing in the world that can keep me from making you my wife. I've just begun to realize that it's more important for you to have your father walk you down the aisle than it is for me to get what I want as soon as possible." The fire popped beside us as Manning tilted his head.

"If it means waiting until you realize it, too, I'm willing to do that."

The idea of my father, who'd wanted nothing to do with me for over a decade, walking me down the aisle was so painful that my nose tingled with unwelcome tears. It would never happen. It wasn't an image I'd been prepared for, and Manning had lobbed it at me without warning. This time, I managed to get up before he could pull me back. "Then I hope you're prepared to wait a while." I covered myself with a throw, tucking it under my arms. "It's not as if I haven't thought about having them there, but I don't see how it would work."

"It's not as impossible as you think," he said, sitting up. "You'll never know if you don't try."

Manning and I had been doing so well. The thought that he'd let anything come between us anymore—especially things we'd already defeated, like my family and his, and the stupidity of perfection—angered me. "You sound like a middle school inspirational poster," I said, hoping it came out as bitchy as I meant it to.

"If you can tell me with complete sincerity that you have absolutely no desire for them to be there, then I'll accept that," he said. "You can't know how badly I want to marry you, and I'm not willing to let them come between us again. But you should know that I'm going to talk to your father before we do this. And Tiffany, too."

I turned to look down at him, my face heating. "How can you go to him for permission? Of course he'll say no. He never wanted us together, and in case you've forgotten, he got his way on that issue for a very long time."

"It's not permission. It's respect."

"Why? Why do you care what they think?"

"Maybe they don't mean anything to you anymore, but they were my family once, too." He scrubbed his hand through his hair. "This is important to me, Lake."

"What *should* be important to you is the fact that you and I lost several years together thanks to him. Thanks to *both of them*. Is that the kind of family you want?"

"I know it's easier to think this is all their fault, but it isn't." He grabbed his underwear, probably sensing our canoodling was done for the night. The way he was headed, he might even be sleeping on the couch. "I made my own decisions back then, and your father had less impact on those decisions than you think."

Definitely the couch. "If you're trying to make me feel better, you're failing miserably," I shot back as I turned to blow out the candles.

"I want you to put this behind you," he said. "Your old man's stubborn, and he's not going to give in."

If I'd known the marriage topic would veer into such dangerous territory as my family, I never would've broached it. Although I held lingering resentment for the fact that my father had gone out of his way to keep us apart, what really angered me was that he couldn't admit to his mistakes, respect my decision not to attend USC, and try to reconcile with me. He'd let a stupid cluster of buildings come between us.

I pulled one pillow from under Manning and then another, tossing them on the couch as I kept my chin high. "So why do I have to be the one to bridge the gap?"

"Because pride isn't a good enough reason to ruin a relationship with the man who raised you—a man who only ever wanted what was best for you."

"I think you're forgetting one thing," I said, holding the throw closed with one hand as I deconstructed Manning's bed of pillows—and our romantic night. "He doesn't want anything to do with me, either. It's not all *my* stubbornness."

"Your dad misses you." He got up and pulled on his underwear. "I've been saying it for years. I'd never encourage you to reconcile with him if I didn't believe that."

I turned to put out the fire, which I'd only done a couple times. I picked up the poker I'd seen Manning use and hesitated. He watched silently, which was almost worse than arguing with me. It was hard to ignore him when he wasn't speaking.

Finally, he came and took the poker from me. "I know how much his rejection hurts you, but I believe he wants to be back in your life as much as you believe he doesn't."

"Then explain to me why he still hasn't been able to pick up the phone. I'm finally on a 'respectable' career path by his standards. Why hasn't that been enough of a reason to reach out?"

"Let me ask you this," Manning said, crossing his arms, "what could Charles possibly say to excuse his behavior the past decade and a half?"

"Nothing."

"I'm sure that's what he thinks as well. Like you, he's convinced there's too big a gulf between you."

"There is." I picked up the dregs of our whisky. "I can't even believe you're bringing this up now. I was so excited to talk about us—our future—and now all I can think about is them. I thought you understood. I thought you were on my side."

"I'm always on your side, Lake, and that's why I'm pushing this. Not because it'd make me happy, even though it would. It's because I want *you* to be happy. You can't hide the fact that you miss your family forever."

"I'm not hiding anything," I said, turning to leave the room. On my way out, I added, "You don't see me asking *you* to reconcile with *your* father so I can have a perfect wedding full of family fun."

As I said it, my throat thickened with the threat of tears. This was not how I'd anticipated the night would go. Now, not only was I embarrassed that I'd asked for a proposal I hadn't received, but I'd also made a huge mistake by mentioning his father. I knew our situations were night and day, but I couldn't help feeling as if Manning was siding with a man who would've preferred Manning and I never met at all.

I was angry, but not with Manning. He and I were solid—we'd moved the stars on our own. *Despite* my dad. For more than a decade, I'd been without the man who'd raised me—he'd gone that long not caring to close the gap between us. He hadn't congratulated me on my graduation from NYU. Hadn't checked in on my life beyond whatever he got from my phone calls with Mom. He'd let pride get in the way of all of that and he'd missed too much of my life. He didn't deserve to come in at the best part.

"Lake," Manning said from behind me as I set our glasses in the sink.

I rubbed the bridge of my nose as I glanced out into the backyard. It was a command to turn around, but I didn't want to face him after what I'd said. I should never have brought his father into this. He was a monster from his core. That wasn't my dad, no matter how he'd hurt me.

I turned to find Manning leaning in the doorway in his underwear, arms crossed over his oiled chest, hair sticking up in all directions. The man was equal parts sexy and cute and wholly impossible to stay angry with.

"I'm sorry," I said, deflating. "I shouldn't have said that."

"It's okay," he said. "I know you didn't mean it that way."

"I just don't understand why this matters so much to you."

"One of the reasons I never touched you was because I knew it would ruin your relationship with your family." His torso expanded with a breath, a frown on his face. "You know if you and I had gotten together, even if Tiffany hadn't been in the picture, it would've created a rift between you and your dad. I can't help feeling this is my fault."

"It isn't, though," I said.

"Regardless if it is or isn't, you and I are older now. *We're* as much adults as they are. If your dad and I have been able to keep in touch, you and he should be able to at least try."

"But I'm happy, Manning. Truly happy—as happy as I could ever get. What gives my dad the right to skip all the hard and scary parts of my life and come in when everything is great?"

"I already told you." Manning crossed the kitchen and slid a hand under my hair, caressing my cheek with his thumb. "This isn't about him. It's about you. And us."

"Are we not okay?" I asked quietly. "Was I wrong to think everything was as close to perfect as it could get?"

"Oh, Birdy," he whispered. "You weren't wrong. I wouldn't change a thing about our life together." He put both palms to my cheeks. "I guess part of me just wanted to give you what I don't have and never will. Maybe, selfishly, *I* want those things back . . . a father, a sibling, even a mother. I don't have them anymore, and it kills me that you don't, either—because of me."

My heart dropped. I had been the selfish one, thinking this was only about me. Manning had needs that'd been easy for me to ignore. "I'm sorry," I said. "I forget that you've lost not only *your* mom and dad, but mine as well. I know you had good times with your family until Maddy's death."

"That was a different life. Maybe I need to let go rather than trying to get you to forgive them. It's my own insecurities bringing all this up."

Having lost any sense of family as a teen, he reminded me all the time that I came first. Him and me, us—we were his priority. I leaned into his touch, sinking into the familiar roughness of his palm. "I'm your family."

"And I don't want to wait any longer to make that official. I want you as my wife—now. I want you pregnant with my child—now."

The abruptness of his words caused heat to bloom from my chest to my face. A minute ago, I'd been concerned he was having second thoughts. Suddenly, we were talking babies? It wasn't as if the idea of children never came up—it did frequently— but there was something extra arousing about his impatience. "You've said that before. Careful, or one of these days, you might wear me down."

He narrowed his eyes on my mouth. "You say that like it's a threat."

"It is. There's no reason we can't start planning a wedding, but we're definitely not ready for a baby."

"Remind me again why not? You graduate in less than six months. If I knock you up now—"

I widened my eyes. "We won't even be married by then."

He shrugged, slipping a firm hand inside the blanket and down my ribs. "So maybe your wedding dress is a little snug around the middle."

"Manning—"

He groaned, walking me back until my ass hit the counter. "You have any idea what that image does to me, you as a pregnant bride?"

Truthfully, it did things to me, too. For years, it'd been our plan to wait until I'd been working a year or two, but that didn't mean I didn't think about it all the time. "I'm supposed to start looking for a job soon."

"There's always a reason for us not to be together, not to get married, not to have a baby," he said, gathering up the throw to expose my thigh. "If we've done nothing else right in our lives, we have bad timing down to an art, so why fight it?"

Manning's fiendish need for a baby excited me, and not just because he was growing hard against my stomach. That happened whenever he went into *protect, provide, mate* mode. But tonight, his impatience made me pause. I needed to know there was no chance Manning needed a baby to fill a hole left by both his family and mine. Manning would never accept an unfilled hole in my soul. I owed him the same. I could give him back a family he'd once had. If I was the only thing keeping him from them, I couldn't be selfish any longer.

Maybe Manning was right about this. He knew the true meaning of a bad father. I'd kept my dad at arm's length for so long and for reasons I wasn't even sure were still important to me. It was hard to hold a grudge when I had the life I'd always wanted. I could've grown up in a household like Manning's. Instead, my parents had done nothing but try to give me every opportunity. As Manning held onto me, his trust in me as solid as ever, I had to admit I'd done wrong by him. I hadn't thought of how deeply all of this impacted him. Not only did I want Manning to be a father, but I wanted him to have one, too. I hadn't acted that way, though. I'd given Manning shit on more than one occasion for keeping in touch with my dad. For too long, I'd pretended as if their relationship was a problem, when the reality was, in Manning's eyes, it was probably a gift.

I sighed heavily, defeat working its way through me. Manning held me close as my body went slack. "What is it?" he asked.

"My mom invited me for Sunday dinner recently."

"Me too," he said. "She does every few months. You tell her no. *I* tell her no."

What was I thinking? I wasn't sure. I only knew if I didn't make a move now, it might be another decade before I worked up the nerve to see them again. And I wasn't waiting that long to marry the man in front of me. "What if he doesn't want to make things right?" I muttered. "What if I go there and my own dad can't even look at me?"

"Then I'll make him look at you. Show him this has gone on too long. I will do everything in my power to mend what's missing in your life, and if I can't, you'll have to be satisfied knowing it'll only be you and me—but it'll *always* be you and me."

I smiled a little. "I suppose I can live with that."

I'd thought many times about contacting my dad; I'd just never considered *actually* doing it. The thought terrified me, but Manning had given me so much over the years, I wanted to do this for him, and for our relationship. And, if I was honest, for myself. I missed my father, regardless of how he'd treated us, and I'd gone long enough on my own. Maybe that should have strengthened my resolve, knowing I could live without him, but I wanted my family back in my life. Not only my dad, but my sister, too, if she and I could ever move past the man between us.

It was time to go home.

4

Standing before my parents' front door, Manning and I were faced with a version of the same welcoming holiday wreath my mother had hung every year of my childhood—crisp greenery offset by a red, poufy felt bow. Like always, the cul-de-sac curved with neat lawns, and LED lights trimmed every roof, even weeks after Christmas. An ocean breeze cooled the back of my neck. Not much had changed in the years since I'd moved away, and yet, everything was different.

Despite the temperate day, my hands reddened from a January chill—and from gripping the two containers of food I'd brought so I wouldn't show up empty-handed.

I didn't even realize I was looking at the neighbor's house Manning had helped build until he turned, too. "What'd we even talk about that day?" he asked, his eyes on the wall where we'd sat.

"I don't know. Little nothings." I glanced up at him. "But at the time it'd felt like the world."

He rubbed the back of my neck, moving my hair aside. I'd cut it to my shoulders the week before. Being thirty-one and on my own for over a decade should've been enough to face my dad feeling like an adult, but I wasn't sure it would be. I hoped looking the part would help him see I wasn't the same girl who'd bowed to her father's every demand.

"I'll go in first," Manning said. "They're expecting me."

"You and a date," I reminded him.

"I only said I was bringing someone to give your mom a heads up for the meal."

I'd been mentally preparing for this for weeks. As it had many times over the drive from Big Bear, my stomach flipped at the thought of walking in uninvited. "Okay," I agreed.

Manning raised his fist to knock, but I pulled his elbow back down. I glanced up at the second-floor landing where I'd sat through many sunsets, watching our neighborhood from the upstairs of the only home I'd known until eighteen. "What if they're disgusted with us?" I asked. "Embarrassed? Maybe we should've called first."

"It's not the kind of thing you say over the phone," he reminded me. "And if that happens, what changes, except that we're finally freed by the truth?"

"My dad's contempt is loud in his silence. It'll be deafening in person."

"Give him a chance." Manning kissed the top of my head. "If he can't accept it, you don't lose anything."

"You do," I said.

"You're more important. If he can't accept that you and I are sincerely happy, then I gave him too much credit."

I turned my entire body to him, hugging the Tupperware so tightly to my stomach, the plastic edges pressed through my sweater. "And what about Tiffany?"

"At least we know what to expect from her." Manning and I had been over this several times, but he patiently walked me through it again. "She'll make it about her, and there'll be a scene. But when she finds something else to be annoyed over, she'll move on."

I shifted between feet. If I was an expert in anything, it was the drama that turned Tiffany's world. The difference now, though? I wasn't an innocent kid enduring her sister's overdeveloped sense of teen angst. I'd crossed lines and made decisions *knowing* they'd hurt her.

But I was also older and more adept at taking shit. I was steeled by the knowledge that nothing Tiffany said or did could deny or undermine the love between Manning and me. Compared to my dad, the approach of Tornado Tiffany actually felt manageable.

Manning knocked firmly, then let himself in. "Hello?"

Once he'd disappeared into the house, I stepped through the open door. Even the warm embrace of home and the festive pine-needle air couldn't strip the tension from my body.

It didn't help that the first door off the entryway shut off my father's study. I could picture him at his desk, doing whatever it was he did in there. Where the study had once held an air of mystery and the forbidden, I no longer cared about it. He'd probably made calls to his mistress in there, corresponded with his friends at the Ritz as he'd arranged the wedding for one daughter and the downfall of his other. Maybe he'd even used his power and influence to get me into USC instead of letting me do it myself—I wouldn't put much past him.

I tiptoed past, trying to quiet my boot heels on the tile. Mom had ripped up the carpet on the stairs to the second floor. More wreaths and poinsettias decorated the house. In the TV room, a real tree stopped a foot beneath the ceiling—it was still full and deeply green, not to mention weighed down with a mixture of expensive glass ornaments and colorful sentimental ones.

The turkey-in-the-oven aroma and deep register of Manning's voice called me to the kitchen like a siren song, but I stayed quiet and out of sight.

"It's been so long since you came by," my mom said. I had to lean forward to listen, her voice soft enough that I assumed she and Manning were hugging. "I left all the decorations up for you. I wasn't sure if you'd spent the holidays with anyone."

"Thank you, Cathy."

"Although . . . well, I haven't mentioned anything to Charles or Tiffany because they'll call me silly. When you said you were bringing a date, I just couldn't imagine you'd introduce us to anyone. It's not the kind of man you are, mixing your two lives. Unless those lives are already . . . mixed."

"Cathy," he said.

"Am I right?" she asked. "If not, it's okay. I want you to be happy, Manning. But I miss my baby and sometimes I lie awake at night wondering if you're the only person who could bring her home."

Chills rose over my skin despite the weight of my sweater. Although this hadn't been my home in a while, it felt nice to hear her say that. No matter what had passed between all of us, I could never erase the happy memories I'd made in this house.

"I know you and Tiffany divorced," Mom continued, "but you're family. We're *your* family. So tell me we haven't seen you in years because you've had a very good reason to stay away."

"It's a good reason, ma'am," Manning said, and I heard both the pride and emotion in his voice. "The best. Almost as good as why I came back."

That was my cue to enter a kitchen I hadn't stepped foot in for years, but where I'd eaten more meals than anywhere, had learned to cook, and had spent countless hours on homework. Some days, between school, Dad's work, Mom's real estate appointments, and Tiffany's social life, the kitchen table was the only time all day I'd see my family in one place.

Still, my feet were leaden in my boots—and my mom was *supposed* to be the easiest part of the day. I peeked into the kitchen and caught sight of Manning's back. Knowing he'd be by my side gave me the courage to do it. I walked in food first, holding out the containers of pie and tamales I'd brought like a shield.

Manning turned at my footsteps, revealing Mom behind him. I realized in that moment that I'd expected to see the same woman who'd raised me—after all, she sounded the same and treated me the same over the phone. In a cardigan and cigarette pants, hair done in a long bob, her style hadn't changed, but it took my brain a moment to close the fourteen-year gap between us. She was thinner, the angles of her jaw and curve of her cheekbones more pronounced.

Her eyes, the same family of blue she'd passed on to Tiffany and me, filled with tears in an instant. "Lake?" she nearly whispered.

My voice broke. "Mom."

She came and hugged me around the food clutched in my hands, not even seeming to notice it between us. It was hard not to fall headlong into her familiar scent, a mixture of lemon dish soap and Chanel No. 5.

Manning carefully took the Tupperware from me, then found spots for it on the crowded countertops. The tension in his fingers and jawline mirrored the stiffness of my shoulders. This was as important to him as it was terrifying to me, which was the catalyst behind why I'd come.

But in the end, it wasn't the reason. *This* was: my mom rubbing my back as I fought the urge to cry, comforting me the way she had so many times growing up.

"Lake, honey. There, there," Mom said. She'd always seemed to know when I was upset, even when I'd hidden it. "You're so grown up. Such a beautiful young woman."

With her soft words and tightening embrace, what became clear was the years I'd taken away from her by feuding with my dad and Tiffany. I'd known that already, and had harbored some guilt over it, but for the first time, I saw everything as Manning always had. My parents and I had missed out on valuable time together over issues that were heavy because I'd given them more weight than they deserved. Unsure of how else to convey a sudden and overwhelming regret, I hugged her back and just said, "Mom."

She pulled back to take my face in her hands. Despite a sheen of tears, she smiled, the corners of her eyes creasing with new wrinkles. "You're my baby, you know that?"

I nodded, my chin wobbling. "Yes."

"Thank you for coming home."

"Thank Manning," I said, already missing his presence. Where had he gone? With a slight turn of my head, all I could manage with my mom's hands holding my cheeks, I saw he hadn't gone anywhere but to a corner where the counters met. The same corner he'd stood the night he'd gotten out of jail, the one spot from where he could see everything in the kitchen, including the doorway to the foyer and to the backyard. He did the same at home, keeping his back to the wall. In public, too. He always walked closest to the curb, insisted on driving any time we were together, and sat at dining tables where he could see the entrance to the restaurant. I hadn't really noticed the habit back then, but it'd become obvious over years of living with him.

Mom kept an arm around me, following my gaze to Manning. "Oh my," she said on a sigh. "I suspected over the years, and even hoped, but I didn't really consider the . . . logistics."

"You hoped?" I asked quietly.

She turned back to me. "That you and Manning had found your way to each other? Yes. After his divorce, of course."

"But why?" I asked.

48

She shook her head, as if she wasn't quite sure herself. "I guess it was the only comfort I had. Manning is such a strong, capable man. And loving, too. It gave me peace thinking he was with you."

It was a nice sentiment, but also a reminder of the fact that my connection with Manning had always been impossible to ignore—and yet they had. Ignored it. All of them. I pulled back, wary of forgetting the past, even though I didn't necessarily want to put more distance between us. "Is it a problem that I'm here?"

"Of course not. I've got plenty of food—"

"I mean for Dad."

Manning rounded the island, taking a beer from the fridge on his way.

"He'll have to accept it or stay in his study all night," she said.

The fear that Tiffany or my dad would walk in stopped me from reaching for Manning's hand. He winked at me, acknowledging that the same was true for him. "What do you want?" he asked. "Wine? Beer? Water?"

"Water's good," I said.

"You should go to the study to say hello," Mom added. "Might be easier for him to swallow this on his territory."

It all had to be on his terms. It wasn't surprising but that didn't mean it wasn't also frustrating. "On second thought," I said to Manning, swallowing as my nerves kicked in, "I'll take some wine."

Manning nodded and left the room, presumably to raid my dad's bar.

Mom picked up an oven mitt. "Almost forgot about the candied yams," she said, opening the oven and waving heat away. "I recreated Christmas dinner in case Manning hadn't gotten one." She looked over her shoulder at me and hesitated. "Has it always been him?"

"Always."

"And is it . . ." She straightened up, moving the baking dish to a trivet. "Is it good?"

I crossed my arms in front of me as the contents of my stomach tumbled. "If he weren't the best thing that ever happened to me," I said, "do you think I'd put all of us through this?"

"Surely not," she agreed, smiling again with tear-glossed eyes, despite my defensive tone.

I inhaled deeply. "About Tiffany—"

Mom waved a mitt at me. "Don't worry about her."

"But—"

"Pinot Noir and a peace offering," Manning said, returning with wine and a tumbler of amber liquid. "He'll be in the mood for this midday."

I took both drinks. "Thanks."

"Want me to come with you?"

"It's okay." Walking into my dad's study after all this time with my sister's ex-husband—a man my dad had tried to keep me from—didn't seem like the right way to approach this.

"I said I'd be by your side the whole time," Manning reminded me.

"Knowing you're here is enough. I should do this alone so he doesn't feel ambushed."

"When you get to the part about you and me, I'd like to be there."

A conversation with my dad wouldn't last long. On his best days, he wasn't one for idle chitchat. The thought of being alone with him beyond formalities was enough to make me shudder. "Give us a few minutes," I said to Manning, "but no longer."

He squeezed my shoulder. "I'll be right outside the door."

If my mom had an opinion on how I should do this, she didn't volunteer it. She just watched as Manning walked me out of the kitchen. Once in the foyer, there was nothing left to do but knock. Since my hands were full, Manning tapped on the door.

"Grab a bottle of bourbon and come on in," came my dad's voice.

"He must've heard me earlier. He thinks you're me." Manning jutted his chin at me, urging me in as he turned the knob. "You've already got the Maker's Mark. Go on."

With a steeling breath, I entered the lion's den armed only with liquid courage and the comforting knowledge that when it came to my relationship with my father, things couldn't get much worse.

5

The door to my dad's study closed behind me, sealing me into a room I knew about as well as the man himself. Quiet, tidy, and eerily still, the room only held things my dad loved. Expensive liquor bottles and crystal glasses. Business textbooks that dated back to his time in school. Guns. File cabinets I'd never seen the contents of—important items that kept our household running but that had been sealed away from the women in his life. It occurred to me that Manning probably knew this office better than I did and had maybe even been privy to its secrets and mysteries.

It took Dad a moment to look up from his computer. With his double take, the beginnings of his smile faded. "What's this?"

Taking him by surprise had been a risk; he didn't like to be caught off guard, but this way, he wouldn't have time to work himself into a fury, either. At least not right away. "I . . . I came for dinner."

He sat back in his seat, looking me over. "I thought you were Manning."

I walked farther into the room and set his bourbon on the desk. Although there were more gadgets, it mostly looked the same. "This is—"

"I know what it is." He picked up the tumbler but didn't drink from it. He had a USC paperweight that had once been on my dresser.

He noticed me looking at it. "What are you doing here?"

"I came for dinner," I repeated. With the way he glowered at the door behind me, I felt the need to add, "Mom didn't know."

"You could've given her some warning. Seeing you must've upset her."

There might not've been a quicker path to making me feel like a child than standing in front of his desk. Here, I'd received summer reading lists, been scolded or praised over grades, and been assigned chores. It wasn't a *bad* feeling so much as a familiar one. Though my dad's study had been intimidating, it'd made me more nervous than afraid—the way he'd click about on his computer, doing what looked like important things as he'd ask about my day at school.

I was a mixture of all those things now—intimidated, nervous, afraid—but the difference was I'd grown up and, for the most part, had learned how to harness those emotions.

And that I was old enough to drink.

I took a long sip of wine and sat across from him. "I didn't come in here to talk about Mom. I came to warn you that I'll be at the dinner table whether you want me there or not."

"*My* dinner table," he said.

"Not just yours. All of ours." He stared at me as if I'd wandered in off the street. Maybe I'd stunned him—my unflinching father. His silence only spurred me on. "Who makes the dinner you *eat* off the table every night?" I asked. "Which little girl has stitches on her chin from when she tripped and hit the edge? Who—"

"All right, all right. I get the gist." He rubbed the bridge of his nose, leaning back in his seat with a heavy sigh. "Give me a minute."

Only when he shut his eyes could I really allow myself to look at him. He, too, was older. Graying at his temples, lines on his face and hands, he wore his age more obviously but more gracefully than my mother, who'd seemed tired.

Didn't he have anything to say? Didn't I look different to him, too?

"Of course you do," he said.

I hadn't realized I'd said it aloud, but if we had any hope at a relationship, it was probably best I started speaking up. There was no reason he should intimidate me anymore. Where he was concerned, I had nothing left to lose. He'd given up hope on me long ago. Not for the first time, I understood my sister's apathy over anything that mattered to my father. If even her best efforts were met with disappointment, why try?

Finally, he opened one eye and then another. "Why now?"

"Why now what?"

"You left with no notice. We haven't seen you in years. Of course I'm going to ask what brings you back."

"I do," Manning said from behind me.

I turned in my seat to look at the man I loved, the one who'd not only brought me back, but *had* my back. I hadn't heard him come in, and maybe I was supposed to do this kind of thing on my own, but I was glad for his reinforcement.

Manning entered, closing the study door behind him. He created his own presence in the room instead of shrinking for my dad the way my sister, mom and I did. His eyes stayed forward as he approached my chair. "Mr. Kaplan."

I sat back, unsurprised to find Dad watching me, even as he said, "Manning . . ."

"He's the reason I'm here," I said.

My dad folded his hands on his desk like he was the president about to address the nation. "I suspect he's to blame for many of the choices you've made."

"He is," I said. "And I'm not ashamed of that."

Dad ignored me, turning his attention to Manning. "What do you expect me to say to this?" he asked him. "I've treated you like a son for a long time now."

"And you have no idea what that's meant to me," Manning said, gesturing to the bar cart. "We've consumed some pretty great fucking liquor in here. Had meaningful discussions. Made plans for the future. I'm man enough to admit having you in my life is important." I glanced up when he paused to find Manning looking down at me. "I've missed that the past few years, but it's the result of the distance you've put between you and your daughter."

"Me?" he asked, calling our attention back. "Lake is the one who left, who never looked back, and who removed this family from her life as if we were some kind of tumor."

Although there was some truth to his words, he had to know, on some level, everything I'd done had come from a place of hurt. No little girl *wants* to be estranged from her dad, but sometimes, it's best.

I stood to be next to Manning. "He wants to be part of this family," I said. "He's helped me realize I want that, too. Again. I never stopped wanting it, but I let anger, and then pride, get in the way."

Silence stretched between us as I waited for my dad to admit he'd done the same. He straightened some papers to the side of his desk, glancing at his computer screen as if he were reading from a script.

"What are you going to say to your sister? How do you expect her to take this news?"

"Don't change the subject," Manning said. "It was easy for me to come here today, but it wasn't for Lake. She's gotten nothing but silence from you in years, yet she came anyway. She deserves your attention."

I had to stop myself from turning to Manning with an open mouth. I'd never really heard anyone speak to my father that way. In fact, Manning was perhaps the only person I'd ever seen stand up to Dad—though, in the past, it'd usually been in defense of Tiffany, not me.

To my surprise, Dad leaned back in his chair and glided a hand in front of himself. "Then say what you have to say, Lake."

What *did* I have to say? I had expected my dad to do most of the talking—or screaming, if I was honest. I was tempted to chug my Pinot, but instead, I cleared my throat. "I'm sorry it's been so long," I said, and it was true. To see how my parents' appearances alone had changed was jarring. They were getting older, and so was I. That wasn't time I could get back. He didn't respond, and I wasn't sure if that made continuing easier or harder. "I thought you knew how I felt about Manning back then," I said. "I thought you wanted him to marry Tiffany simply because it would hurt me."

"You thought correctly," he said with a firm nod. "Not that I wanted to hurt you, of course. But as my daughter, I knew what was best for you, and I knew you better than you thought I did. I saw in your eyes what you were willing to give up for a man much older than you. One who could never, in my eyes, be worthy of you."

Hearing the truth both saddened and angered me. He'd had no right to decide my future like that. To put Manning in that box, when there was no man worthier, more deserving, of my love. I opened my mouth to tell him so, but Manning took my free hand. He shook his head at me. "Let him speak."

"I had a feeling," my dad continued, his eyes conspicuously on our laced fingers, "if Manning left town, you would follow. If Manning waited until you'd turned eighteen, then he would've gone to school with you, and your studies would've suffered. The only thing that could keep you away from him was your sister."

Since enough time had passed, I was able to see the logic of an overprotective father. I had no doubt *Manning* would do anything to keep his future children safe. And, it was true—I'd been a sixteen-year-old girl blinded by my adoration of a man. Even understanding all that, the truth of the matter still hurt. I glanced into my wineglass, shaking my head. "But Manning and I lost *years* together."

Dad set his elbows on his desk and opened his hands. "I won't apologize for my actions. I did what I thought needed to be done, and I would do it again." Finally, he lifted his eyes to look at Manning. "You may not believe me, Lake, but Manning knows this is true—I only ever wanted the best for you."

I'd had years to come to terms with those truths. I already knew them. I hadn't quite made peace with them, but they didn't shock me. It was a small vindication, having my suspicions confirmed, but not much more. "I believe you," I said, "but I don't know how to forgive you for that—or for casting me aside so easily."

Dad turned his head, looking at his bar cart against one wall, but seemingly lost in a thought. "I understand."

My heart squeezed in my chest. It wasn't as if I'd expected him to beg for forgiveness or even apologize for his behavior. A small part of me had, however, hoped he'd want this reconciliation at least a little bit. Without meaning to, I clutched Manning's hand.

"I'm going to marry her," Manning said.

That snapped both my and my dad's attention back to Manning. "Excuse me?" Dad asked.

"I came to let you know, and to ask for your blessing," Manning continued.

"My *blessing*?" Dad asked, sounding uncharacteristically surprised. "How come?"

"Because I respect you, and because your opinion means more to me than anyone's outside of Lake's and Henry's. We're going to marry with or without your approval, but it would mean a lot to me—and to Lake, I think—if you were there."

Dad sniffed. "What makes you think I'd even consider that? That I would do that to Tiffany?"

"I might let you shame me into feeling bad if I thought your concern for Tiffany was genuine," I said.

"It is," Dad said to me. "Apparently you think I'm something of a monster, but I'm not. Your sister is my first born, my blood. Regardless of how you see things, I love her. She's been through a lot. All of which you've missed."

"But *I* have been there every step of the way," Manning interjected. "I know you care about Tiffany. You know *I* care. You said I was a good husband to her. Am I wrong to say after all you and I have been through, that you trust my judgment?"

After a tense moment, my dad nodded for Manning to continue. "You're not wrong."

"Sir, I love Lake. I have for longer than I'd like to admit, but hiding it from her and you and even myself only did everyone in the family a disservice." He squeezed my hand. "I'm trying to do the honorable thing by bringing this to light."

My heart pounded. This was a moment sixteen years in the making—our 'coming out' in a sense. We'd been inseparable for years, but we might as well have been sixteen and twenty-three again, standing before my menacing father and asking his permission to love each other. I was thankful not to be that girl now, because she wouldn't have walked out of this room with Manning—but *I* would, no matter my dad's response. "I feel the same," I said. "It has always been Manning for me."

"And Lake for me," Manning echoed. "Like you, I've only ever tried to do the best by her, to love and protect her—and now I can do it with every fiber of my being. Without worrying about what anyone else says or thinks."

My dad worked his jaw side to side as his eyes clouded. Though I feared his reaction, it wasn't enough to get me to back down. Not with Manning at my side.

And my father certainly didn't intimidate Manning. "She's my only concern," Manning continued, "my only priority, and I'm here to tell you that you don't need to worry about her anymore. She's safe and happy and cared for."

My dad had clenched his mouth shut, his lips a bloodless line. Anger darkened his face. I couldn't understand how any of what Manning had professed could upset him. I opened my mouth to defend Manning's love for me, and mine for him, with a ferocity my father had never seen. But I stopped when I saw the tears in his eyes.

He set his elbow on the desk and hid his face with one hand. Was he *crying*? "Go," he said after a moment. "Leave."

I'd read the emotion on his face as anger because sadness was so unfamiliar there. I was too surprised to do anything other than let Manning pull me out of the study. Once we were alone in the hallway, I looked up at him. "What just happened in there?"

"He cracked a little—and that's good. Believe me."

"I don't even know what that was."

"Regret. Pain. You're his daughter, Lake. Of course he worries about you with an intensity neither of us will understand until we have our own children." He glanced at the door behind me. "All I did was relieve him of a worry that has weighed on his shoulders for years."

I couldn't help getting choked up, mostly because my emotions were all over the place. Even though I was touched, my pride was still wounded. "If that's true, then why'd he kick us out?"

"It's probably hard for him to let you see him that way." Manning reached for my Pinot, so I handed it over, even though he rarely drank wine. Maybe he'd been more nervous than I'd thought. "I've learned a lot from your dad," he said after a sip, "including the fact that I hide my vulnerabilities from the people I love the same way he does."

"You don't do that with me anymore," I said. Manning would never be able to help being protective of me and our life, but now we made decisions *together* that affected us, including the one to be here today. He'd come a long way from the days of keeping me in the dark with the misguided intentions of protecting me.

"Like I said, I've learned from him," Manning said. "Shutting down his emotions helps nothing and only hurts the people he loves."

"That doesn't explain why he told us to go," I said, still stung by the rejection. "Is he angry?"

"If I had to guess . . ." The corner of Manning's mouth quirked, and after a moment, he chuckled. "I'd say yes—only because *angry* is your dad's default emotion. But I'm sure it's more that he didn't want you to see his concern and regret. That's the way he's programmed. I think we got through to him, though."

"*You* did," I said, raising my hand to touch Manning's cheek. "I've never seen him back down to anyone but you."

"Because I'm more like him than I sometimes want you to realize." He focused his full attention on me, and demanded the same *from* me, so I noticed as his eyes subtly set with determination. "But I promise, the mistakes he's made, the ones my dad's made, and even my own, too, will only serve as lessons to me. They'll shape the father I become for the better."

My stomach fluttered the way it always did at the thought of Manning as a father. This time, though, the butterflies were more severe. Because I knew Manning could already *be* a father. We'd ceremoniously thrown away my birth control after our marriage talk and had already started the process of turning the *idea* of a family into reality.

I curled my fingers a little into Manning's cheek. "Then I don't regret a thing," I said. "If any of our heartache will make us better parents, I have nothing but gratitude for it."

"Same." He winked. "But enough with the difficult lessons. I'm ready to put what I've learned into practice."

So was I. A small part of me wanted to get pregnant quickly, before one of us realized we'd gotten the order of things all wrong. We'd only been at it weeks—but I couldn't help hoping that was all it would take.

6

Even after years away, I moved seamlessly around the kitchen with my mom. She handed me the turkey roast from the oven that she'd made many times throughout my childhood, then complimented my tamales, even though they were a completely untraditional dish for my family.

As I washed my hands, I watched Manning in the backyard through the window over the sink. A cigarette stuck in the corner of his mouth, he squatted to fix an uneven patio chair. When he and I had first moved in together, I'd been able to coax him away from his pack-a-day habit with baked goods, blowjobs, and backrubs. After that, I rarely saw him with a cigarette. But he'd lit up between every meal yesterday, on the drive down today, and now—had he been smoking the entire half hour he'd been in the backyard?

"Always needs to keep his hands busy, that one," Mom said as she moved pots and pans into the sink. "Especially when he's nervous."

Manning had been smoking and moving around non-stop the past few days. Confronting my family might have been his idea, but that didn't mean it was easy for him. "You can tell?" I asked.

"Sure. He's spent a lot of time around here. I wouldn't say he's easy to read all the time, but he has his moods." She smiled a little at me. "Wouldn't you be nervous in his position?"

Manning hadn't seen much of Tiffany since their divorce, although they spoke now and then. I never stayed in the room for their conversations, but according to him, they didn't cover much more than formalities. Manning didn't like hiding our relationship from the people he cared about any more than I did.

Manning moved from a patio chair to what looked like a busted wall sconce. I was still standing at the window when the front door opened and the telltale click of heels crossed the foyer. It happened so quickly that I didn't have time to call for Manning or even my mother, who had disappeared into the pantry.

I seized the nearest bottle of wine and was already pouring myself a refill as Tiffany walked in. She stopped when she saw me, and I froze mid-pour.

Just the island sat between us. Her hair, long and curled, covered the shoulders of a burgundy shrug, and she held a pie tin in her hand. She glanced at my blueberry pie on the countertop and then at me. "You're spilling wine."

"*Shit.*" I set down the bottle and ripped off a paper towel to mop up the overflow.

"I didn't know you'd be here tonight," she said. Her short black dress and high heels wouldn't normally have been out of the ordinary, except that as far as she knew, it was plain old dinner with the family—and Manning and his date.

"Well, I am," I mumbled, glancing over my shoulder at Manning, who'd left me high and dry when this had been *his* idea. I willed him to look up and come inside, but he continued to tinker with the lighting fixture.

Tiffany followed my gaze. This wasn't exactly how I wanted her to find out—I'd assumed Manning would be at my side when she showed up. Even my mother was taking an unusually long time in the pantry. Or maybe, to make things extra uncomfortable, time had slowed down only for Tiffany and me.

Her eyes darted from the window back to my face. "You're here with him?" she asked.

It'd been years since I'd shown up at Manning's home in Big Bear and stayed for good. Even longer since he and Tiffany had decided to end their marriage. But I supposed there was really no amount

69

of time that would make this conversation any less awkward, so I took a steeling breath and raised my overfilled wineglass before I said, "Yes, I'm Manning's, well, *date*—for lack of a better word."

She gagged like a cat with a fur ball stuck in its throat. "Oh my God."

"Yep." I slurped Pinot off the top. "I didn't know the best way to tell you, just that I wanted to do it in person." After setting the glass down, I patted the corners of my mouth with the towel. "I know it's shocking, but believe me, neither of us wants to hurt you."

"You're dating my ex-*husband*," Tiffany pointed out, her voice pitching.

"You have every right to be angry and hurt," I said, opening the cupboard under the sink to toss the paper towel in the trash, "but you have to admit that some part of you knew this could happen."

"How long has this been going on?"

"A long time—but then, you knew that."

I held my breath in anticipation of my sister's wrath. So much time had passed, and so many confusing emotions and memories still tinged the air between us with tension. When Tiffany had asked Manning to the fair all those years ago, could she have ever imagined things would end up this way? Could *I*? And if so, would either of us have changed anything? Because I knew I was in the wrong, and that the insecurity that lived in my sister often caused her to lash out, I wanted to go to her. Hug her. Be her little sister again. Remind her that I loved her despite everything, even as I knowingly hurt her. But this moment wasn't about me—it was about what *she* needed.

"Manning and I want to be a part of this family," I continued when she didn't respond. "We want to stay for dinner and hear about your life—and share ours as well." Again, I looked out the window. After the struggle it'd taken to get me to the house, Manning wouldn't want to leave, but in that moment, I wasn't sure I had any right to force my presence on Tiffany.

Her face scrunched as if she'd bitten into a lemon. "It's weird," she said. "And kind of gross. *I* wouldn't want somebody else's sloppy seconds, especially my sister's, but it's your life."

I blinked at her a few times, trying to process her words. Weird? Gross? Sloppy seconds? I had to stop myself from laughing. That response didn't faze me at all. I'd never seen Manning as sloppy seconds, only as the man I loved. "You're not angry?" I asked.

Tiffany set her pie down. I fought myself from checking if she'd also brought Manning's favorite flavor. She twisted her lips as if considering whether she should be angry. It was unlike her to deny an opportunity to overreact, which made me wonder if she'd matured at some point over the past decade, or if I'd stumbled into some kind of alternate universe. The latter seemed more likely.

"I'm not angry," she decided, lightly flipping some hair over her shoulder. "I mean, I've suspected this since the divorce. I know you told me at the viewing party you hadn't seen him, but I wasn't sure if I could believe you."

"It was the truth," I said. "Nothing happened until after."

"Well, I didn't know that, so all this time, I sort of assumed you might be together." She rounded the island to pick up the wine bottle, checking to make sure I'd left some. "But even if I hadn't had time to come to terms with it," she said, pouring herself a glass, "I don't think the two of you together ever surprised me. Not at camp, and not in New York."

Her point wasn't lost on me. Perhaps Manning and I hadn't always been fair to Tiffany, but it would be impossible to explain or reason away a love like ours. So instead, I just laid out the truth. "If it helps, it was never about hurting you. But Manning and I . . . we are, and always have been, so in love."

She set her drink on the island and squatted to a cabinet to remove a cake stand—the same one my mom and I had used over the years for dessert. It was bizarre to picture Tiffany baking, but apparently, it wasn't her first time. "Oh, I *totally* understand."

Of all the reactions I'd expected to get from Tiffany, *understanding* was nowhere near the top of the list. It wasn't even *on* the list. "You do?" I asked, failing to hide my surprise.

Smiling to herself, she ran her fingers under the lid of the tin, working it open. "Love makes you do crazy things."

Was she serious, or passive-aggressively insulting me? "Yes, it does," I said. "And I know this can't be easy for you, but like I said, neither Manning nor I had any intention of—"

"All right already," she said. "I don't care. This whole thing is, like, ancient history. I have more important things happening in my life."

"Oh." Well, that was different. Or was it? Only one thing could distract Tiffany from talking about herself—and that was talking about herself. "What's . . . happening in your life?"

She opened a draw to get a pie server. "I met a man. A *doctor.*"

"You're dating someone?" I asked.

"Dating?" She hummed a laugh as if enjoying an inside joke. "It seems like such a small word for what we're doing."

She'd just used the same word to describe Manning and me, so of course I understood how small it felt. He and I had done a lot but we hadn't truly *dated.* Certainly that would be lost on Tiffany, though, especially because it seemed as if she'd forgotten I was even in the room. "Who is he?" I asked.

She transferred the pie to the cake plate. "Robby. You don't know him, but he's the most wonderful man I've ever met. He's tall and handsome. And a doctor."

"You mentioned that."

"Well, it says so much about who he is. Kind, caring, and great with kids . . ." She shifted her eyes over my shoulder and out the back window. I couldn't help wondering if Robby really existed in all his perfection, or if this was another way for Tiffany to get a leg up on me. I was in love? She was in *more* love. I'd met the best man in the world? Well, hers was a *doctor*.

Even with the adoring look on her face, I wasn't entirely sure it was genuine. It couldn't be easy to see me with Manning. Was she talking Robby up to make herself look better? Or was she so enamored, she really *didn't* give a shit what we did?

"I'm happy for you." I relaxed my hip against the counter. "How long have you been together?" I asked with a sip of Pinot.

"Over a year. I've never been happier. I literally don't even care about stupid stuff anymore, you know? Robby always says drama is below us."

I nearly spit out my wine. But without drama, who was my sister? "I need to meet Robby."

"He's wonderful," Mom said, reentering the kitchen.

I eyed her armfuls of canned goods. "You felt a sudden need to clean out the pantry?"

"I remembered that Robby asked me to donate some food to a drive at the hospital," she said, averting her eyes.

"*Right.*" Surely, it had nothing to do with wanting to stay out of the fray. I looked for Manning again as Tiffany brushed by me.

"I should say hello," she said, pulling open the sliding glass door.

I started to follow her when my mom touched my arm. "Give them a minute, sweetie."

"Manning might need me there."

"You did it on your own," Mom said. "So can he. Let your sister process this how she needs to."

Reluctantly, I returned to the window to watch them. "Is Robby real?" I asked.

She laughed. "Completely. He's a very nice man. And a doctor! He's patient with her—just what she needs."

"Hmm." I gripped the sink as Manning blew on a dusty light bulb, then screwed it back in. He paused and turned as Tiffany approached. They exchanged a few words, and then he offered her a cigarette, cupping his hand around her mouth as he lit it for her. Tiffany's shoulders fell from around her ears as she cocked a hip. Manning took a drag, smiling a little as he nodded and blew smoke into the backyard. No longer in the same room as Tiffany, relief filtered through me, and it looked as if she felt the same.

She nudged his shoulder with a laugh, then glanced in my direction. Even though Manning and I had ended up together, and I couldn't feel anything other than grateful for it, Tiffany had shared one experience with Manning I still hadn't.

I turned away from the window to face the pies. "Do you have another cake plate?"

"I don't," Mom said, frowning. "Sorry, honey. We'll get both on the table tonight, though."

I lifted the cover and inspected Tiffany's baking skills. Apple—Manning's second favorite flavor. It smelled amazing. "This isn't store-bought?" I asked.

"I'd be surprised. Tiffany loves to bake."

"There's a sentence I never thought I'd hear." I re-covered the dessert. I'd always considered the kitchen *my* domain, but it looked like if I came home again, I'd be sharing it.

Manning slid open the kitchen door for Tiffany, who removed her shrug on her way out of the kitchen.

Noticing my half-empty glass, he picked up the bottle of wine I'd been drinking from the last half hour on his way over to me. "You good?" he asked under his breath.

"I think so."

"Yeah?" he asked, refilling my drink. "Did it not go well? She was weirdly calm out there."

"No, she was fine. I was so shocked that I'm not even sure I remember what we talked about. But . . ."

"Dinner's ready. Go tell your father." Mom paused while separating dinner rolls into a basket, as if suddenly recalling this wasn't just another Sunday dinner. "Never mind. I'll get him."

Once Manning and I were alone, he asked, "But what? What's the matter?"

"It's strange to see you and Tiffany together. She seems so comfortable with you."

He set down the bottle and took my jaw in one big hand, lifting my face to him. "That's good, Lake. Trust me, I've never seen her like this, and I would know—she's in love."

"With a doctor," I added.

He laughed. "Yeah. She doesn't give a rat's ass about us beyond making sure we know what he does for a living. She isn't looking to cause us any trouble."

As he leaned in for a kiss, I checked that we were still alone. "That's probably not appropriate," I told him.

"Lake," he said in the same firm but exasperated tone he used whenever I pulled away from him.

"You can wait until we're home."

With a frown, he let me go. "If I can't kiss you, then you better tell me what I want to hear."

"I love you," I said. "Isn't putting myself through this evidence of that?"

"Hate having to keep my fucking hands off you. It's like I'm twenty-goddamn-three all over again."

Despite his earnest expression, I couldn't help laughing. "It really is funny if you think about it, us being here."

"Hilarious." He stuck his hands in his pockets as my dad entered the kitchen with Mom and Tiffany trailing behind him.

"Hmm," Dad said, circling the island. "Pie . . ."

I figured that was the best I could hope for. He wasn't red in the face or kicking us out or locking himself in his study—not yet, anyway. "With blueberries," I added.

"With *apples*," Tiffany said.

"In the same pie?" he asked.

Tiffany's giggle caused one to bubble up in me as well, but I swallowed it down, still unsure of how to read everyone's mood.

"No, Daddy," Tiffany said, fluttering her lashes. "I made apple, Lake brought blueberry. You have to choose."

He grunted before leaving the kitchen. I knew before I heard the *clink* of glass on glass in the den that he was pouring himself a drink. "Well, go on," he called, as if he could sense our unease from the next room. "Let's sit and eat your mother's dinner."

"Robby *loves* apple pie," Tiffany said. She and I gravitated right to our regular seats at the table, as if no time had passed. "That's why I made it."

"He's coming tonight?" I asked.

"No. We were walking out the door when he got a page. He's on call *a lot*."

"What kind of doctor is he?" Manning asked, setting my refilled wineglass in front of me.

"A pediatrician," she quipped. "Did I not mention that?"

A-*ha*. Patience was a requirement of Robby's *job*. "No wonder," I said.

She narrowed her eyes at me. "What's that mean?"

"Nothing," Manning answered for me, helping me scoot my chair closer to the table before he sat. "He must like kids."

"He does," she said. "It's all he can talk about."

Manning put an arm around the back of my chair. One thing he'd asked of me today was that I didn't talk about our decision to have children. He liked that it only belonged to us for now, and I agreed. By the way he squeezed my shoulder, he must've known what was coming.

"Oh, *grandbabies*," my mom gushed as she carried dishes into the dining room. She waited until my dad was at the table to place one in front of him.

"What the hell are those?" he asked.

"Your daughter made it," she said as she returned to the kitchen. "Something different to spice up our table."

"They're tamales," I said.

"Mexican food?" Dad asked. "You brought them?"

"You don't have to eat them," Tiffany said to him. "But they actually look pretty good."

"I'm with Robby, you know," Mom said, floating back into the room with the roast. "I can't wait for both of you girls to have babies."

"Well, it shouldn't be far off." Dad picked up the carving knife. "Manning here has just asked for my blessing to marry Lake."

7

With my eyes on my empty plate, I couldn't tell if the silence following my dad's declaration was surprise or something else. Announcing our impending wedding was part of the reason we were here, but I'd assumed Manning would be the one to bring it up.

Manning cleared his throat. "I want nothing more than to marry Lake," he said. "She's practically my wife already. It's just a matter of making it official, and we'd love for you all to be there."

Tiffany snorted. "This is beyond twisted. You know that, don't you?"

I looked at Manning as he shrugged, then to my sister. I sat up a little straighter. "It is what it is."

"Goodness." Mom passed rosemary-roasted potatoes to Tiffany. "Charles, serve the turkey."

He stood and slid the roast in front him. "Who wants a leg?" he asked and flipped on the electric knife.

My mom frowned as she started the rotation of side dishes. "That's big news after barely hearing from you for so long," she yelled as my dad carved.

"I know." I accepted a bowl of broccoli. "I'm sorry it's sudden for you, but it isn't for us."

"We don't even know what your life is like." Mom hesitated. "I thought you were living in Pomona."

"Part of the week. On weekends and holidays, I go home."

"What?" Dad sliced off breast meat. "Home?"

"To Manning," I enunciated. "And our place in Big Bear."

My dad turned to Manning, pointing the whirring knife in his direction. After a few tense seconds, he shut it off. "All these years?"

"I would've mentioned it sooner, sir," Manning said, "but Lake and I needed our privacy."

"That's fine. All fine." Dad shrugged. "Makes no difference to me."

Except it *did*. His play of indifference wasn't convincing. Frustrating as it was that he couldn't own up to his feelings, it also made me grateful I'd come today. I hadn't wanted to do this, but I could see my dad cared about his relationship with Manning, just as Manning did. "Manning is the reason I'm here tonight," I said, serving myself a tamale. "Your approval means a lot to him. He wants to be part of this family again."

"We know that, honey," Mom said, taking my hand across the table. "We know you want that, too, and I promise it makes us nothing but ecstatic. Of course you have our blessing—"

"Cathy."

"*What*, Charles?" She barely spared him a glance before continuing. "I wouldn't miss the wedding for the world. I want to be part of it, though. I—*we*—want to know more about who you are now."

I went stiff. I didn't know where to begin, or how to get things back to what they were—yet my mom looked at me expectantly, waiting for me to spill my guts. "Right *now*?" I asked.

"Let's start with having a nice meal together tonight," Manning said, one arm back around my chair as he accepted a platter of sliced turkey with the other. "We'll go from there."

Grateful for the save, I put my hand on Manning's thigh, even though it also meant eating one-handed. "We don't need an answer now," I said.

"We just wanted to let you know our plans," Manning added.

"Let's see the ring," Tiffany said.

I'd told Manning I'd wear the mood ring for now, knowing how he worried about money. I didn't need more than that anyway. I doubted Tiffany would understand, though, so I said, "We're putting that money into the wedding."

"No *ring*?" she asked. "Are you serious?"

"If your sister doesn't want a ring, that's fine," my mom said, batting her lashes at Manning. "But it *is* a nice symbol of your devotion to each other, even if it's something small."

"I'll take that into consideration," Manning said.

"How's school?" Dad asked just as I had taken a bite—not that he'd notice since he continued to look anywhere but at me.

Still, it was akin to me taking a step into this house. Dad was opening a door long closed, not only accepting my presence but inviting me in. Swallowing my food with a sip of water, I shivered when Tiffany's knife scraped the china. "It's great," I said. "By this time next year, I'll be a licensed vet."

"She's one of the top students in her program," Manning said.

"I should hope so." Dad cut his turkey breast, nodding. "She'll be thankful for years of focused study when she's slicing Fido open on her operating table."

"*Dad*," Tiffany said, making a face.

"What?" he asked. "You better get used to it if you're going to marry a doctor."

"Marry?" Tiffany perked up, grinning. "Did Robby say something to you?"

"No," Dad barked. "You remind me at every Sunday dinner that you plan to be married by the end of this year."

She put an elbow on the table and her chin in her hand. "I do."

As cautious as I was about rejoining this family, there was some comfort in their bickering. My dad was still unapologetically himself, but at the root of it, he cared.

"Anyway," I continued, "I'll spend the next few months interviewing with a couple animal hospitals in Big Bear, but eventually I want to open my own practice."

He raised his tumbler. "What you should've been doing from the start," he said.

"Maybe," I conceded. "I just had to figure that out on my own."

Dad continued eating. He didn't smile at that, but his frown eased completely. "We're not paying for the wedding," he said, looking between my sister and me. "Either one."

Money hadn't even crossed my mind. I'd thought getting him to acknowledge our presence long enough to hear there *was* a wedding would be the one and only topic on tonight's agenda.

"I'll be fine," Tiffany said. "I learned my lesson the first time thinking money wasn't as important as love. Not having it can cause major problems." She popped a potato in her mouth. "That's why I made finding a wealthy man a priority! I never realized I could have both."

I studied my sister's body language—her contented sighs, tiny smiles, the pink tinge of her cheeks—to decide whether she was bluffing about her relationship. "I could've told you years ago you needed someone with money," I said.

"As could I," Manning added. "And I did. Several times."

Tiffany shrugged off our comments. Manning, on the other hand, forked a broccoli stem so hard, it tumbled over the side of the plate. His heavy brows made me wonder if Tiffany had hurt his feelings by implying he hadn't financially supported her the way she'd needed. Though her comment had been rude and thoughtless, I hadn't thought she still had the power to get under his skin.

Turning back to the table, I said, "We're fine to pay for our wedding. Money isn't an issue for us. The ceremony will be pretty small and intimate—" I glanced at Manning when he removed his arm from the back of my chair. "But even if it wasn't, we'd be fine. Manning's furniture sells very well."

"Even in this economy?" Dad asked.

Manning cleared his throat. "I do fine."

"That's what I was saying." I tried to catch his gaze, but he kept it forward. "You have more business than you know what to do with."

"Then you've got a solid empire there. Men my age are losing their jobs—and savings—with this recession." Dad scratched his jaw. "I've been telling you for years you need help."

"I have help. Some local kids."

After our talk weeks ago, Manning had relented and taken on the teenaged son of a contractor he knew to help keep the shop organized. Then, he'd hired a twenty-year-old college student to do his books. "I think Dad means someone to help with the actual furniture."

"I have an ear to the ground, but I'm sure it'll be a while before I find anyone."

"Maybe I can help," Dad said. "E-mail me a job description and the hourly wage."

Manning ran a finger under his collar. "I'm not sure it's the right time. Who knows when the economy will recover?"

"I think we've survived the worst of it," I said.

"My furniture is a luxury, not a necessity. And with a business directly related to homes, in this market, things could still decline."

I could hear the irritation in Manning's voice, though I wasn't sure where it was coming from. Even if business did suffer, Manning had always been good with money. I had complete faith we'd land on our feet. Didn't he?

"Maybe it's time to consider reducing the quality of the pieces," Dad suggested. "With some cheap labor, you could create a more affordable line."

Manning wiped his mouth with his napkin and set it on the table before scooting out his chair. "Excuse me."

"Where are you going?" I asked, twisting my head to try to read his body language.

"To get something from the truck," he said on his way out of the dining room. "I'll be right back."

I wasn't buying that, and neither was my mom. "Why do you get on him about his business?" Mom asked my dad. "You know he likes to do things his way."

"Because he's being stubborn for no good reason. If he's planning on a family, he needs to think smarter about how to generate the most income while keeping expenses down."

Manning struggled with that part of his business. Building each piece to his nearly impossible specifications kept him from looking for help, but he also felt pressured to not only take on—but please—every client.

"He's doing everything the way he needs to," I said, also getting up. "He'd never hire cheap labor to make an extra buck. Also, he's more dedicated than anyone I know, and he has a loyal customer base to show for it."

"I didn't say anything about dedication," Dad called after me as I left the room. "I'm talking about basic supply and demand here."

I took my jacket from the coatrack and pulled it on as I went out front. With the setting sun as his backdrop, Manning leaned against the side of his truck, smoking. Again. I bypassed the front walkway for the lawn's grassy hill, which got me to him faster. "What's the matter?" I asked.

"Nothing, beautiful."

I crossed my arms. "Then stop smoking so much."

"It's just a little more than usual," he said but dropped the half-finished cigarette to the curb. He stamped it out, nodding at me. "See? Now come here."

I went to him, hugging his middle as I looked up at him. "What's wrong, Manning? Really? I've seen your books. We did our tax returns together. I know we're not having money trouble."

"We easily could be. With your tuition and a wedding and starting a family on top of the mortgage and business expenses—Lake, your dad's right. I've hit a ceiling with how much I can produce. I could be making a lot more."

I shook my head. "We're fine. We're in less debt than most people and we only have it in the first place because of my student loans. I'm graduating soon, and I can start contributing. Plus, I still have some money saved from when I worked on the show."

"Money you set aside for our baby's future." He smoothed a hand over my hairline. "I don't want you to worry about any of this. We *are* fine. We're perfect."

As he said it, I rubbed the frown lines from between his eyes. Worry was stitched into Manning's DNA. "There's no such thing as perfect."

"As long as you exist, your argument will fall on deaf ears."

"I'll support whatever you decide," I said. "I love that you're so dedicated to your craft, but I also worry you work yourself too hard. If you hire help, it means you can spend more time with me."

"It also means being responsible for someone else's income. If the economy tanks even more, then what?"

"You fire him."

"He—or she—would depend on me. I'd only bring on someone skilled, not someone I could just let go when times are tough." He sniffed. "By the way, I would never make an 'affordable line.'"

"I forbid you from it."

"Oh yeah?"

"Yep. You're too good at what you do. It would devalue your work." I patted the rectangular pack in his back pocket. "And while we're at it, I also demand that you cut back on the smoking before you get in too deep again."

He covered the top of my head with his hand. "This little girl thinks she can forbid me from anything."

"I'm not so little anymore," I said, straightening up.

"No, you're not." He laced his hand with mine and pulled me away from the truck. But as I turned back for the house, he tugged me in the opposite direction. "Come with me."

"Where?" I asked as we walked off the curb and toward my parents' neighbor's house.

He didn't answer, walking us along their front lawn until we were standing at the end of their walkway. He released my hand to point at the wall we'd both sat on the day we'd met. "I can still see you standing in front of me, that giant backpack weighing you down. And then, up on the wall, nervously kicking the heels of your tennis shoes against the bricks."

"What makes you think I was nervous?"

"Call it a hunch."

I smiled, sticking my hands in the back pockets of my jeans. Summers didn't have that same breezy, careless feel anymore. They were different now, but so were Manning and I.

He'd been right when he'd said we'd both been kids back then. To me, he'd been as much an adult as anyone else I knew, but the truth was, he'd been as young and unsure of himself as I'd been. That Pink Floyd shirt he'd worn had been so old, it would've been impossible to keep it around, but I wished he still had it. I'd never forget that image of him sitting with a cigarette in the corner of his mouth as he'd assessed me with a curious, albeit restrained, gaze.

"Ready to go back in?" he asked.

Lost in the memory, I hadn't noticed him leave my side. I turned to find him a few feet back, as if he'd started for the house without me.

"Sure."

"Don't forget your jewelry," he said, a twinkle in his eye.

91

"Ha-ha," I said, showing him the bracelet on my wrist. "You wish I'd lose it again, just so you could be the hero and find it."

"I'm serious." He nodded at my feet. "You dropped something."

As I glanced down, a glint of gold caught the light of the lowering sun. I stooped, about to pick up what looked like a piece of jewelry, but froze. A ring shone against the pavement, centered with a pearly, iridescent stone surrounded by diamonds. Although it looked valuable, its uniqueness struck me first, that awful feeling of losing something sentimental. "This isn't mine, but it's beautiful," I said.

He bent down and dusted it off. I barely caught the suppressed smile on his face before I noticed he was on one knee. I gasped, covering my mouth as my eyes watered. "Manning—what . . .?"

"I wasn't planning this or anything," he said. "Been carrying it around for a while, and I definitely didn't think I'd do this at your parents' of all places."

I kept my hand over my mouth, nodding, even though I struggled to make sense of what he was saying.

"This is a moonstone." He held up the ring. "Over time, the color can subtly change. It's not the most expensive stone or the most traditional. It's kind of like the adult version of a mood ring. See how the edges aren't smooth?"

The stone took a natural shape, oval but still misshapen, highlighted by the tiny diamonds around the outside edge. I nodded.

"I didn't just pick the most expensive ring," he said. "I wanted one that reminded me of you."

Finally, I lowered my hands, dropping onto my knees. "Are you asking me to marry you? Why are you talking so much?"

He laughed. "Nerves, I guess."

"You know my answer, Manning."

He took my hand in both of his and removed our cherished mood ring from my fourth finger. "I love you, Lake. I guess there are lots more romantic places I could ask you to be mine, but where better than the first spot I laid eyes on you?"

Manning had to have known proposing in a place painted with our history would mean more to me than anything else. I nodded hard. "I love you, too."

"In this spot, you opened your beautiful mouth and decided to trust me. To love someone you weren't supposed to. To ask me about Pink Floyd." He smiled. "So I'd really like if, right here, you'd agree to be my wife."

"I do," I said, bumbling over the words with a fluttered laugh. "I mean *yes*. 'I do' comes later."

"Officially, even though I already think of you as mine forever—will you marry me?"

How could I possibly explain how much I wanted that, too? Had always wanted that? What could I say to convey my love for him? "Manning—"

"Just say yes, Birdy."

My eyes watered. Though I'd fought with Manning many times over the fact that perfection didn't exist, in the end, I might've actually been wrong about that. A tear crept down my cheek. "Yes."

He slid the ring in place and stood, helping me up. I launched myself into his arms and he pulled me against him so tightly, I was off my feet, our mouths meeting. "You went awfully far to get me to kiss you at my parents' house," I whispered against his lips.

"Not far enough if you ask me." He pecked me and set me down. "Let's get back inside before they come looking for us."

"Do we have to?" I sighed as he took my hand and walked us up the walkway. I lifted our interlocked hands to inspect the ring. "It's beautiful. I don't want to share it with anyone."

He released my hand, took the ring off, and tucked it into a black velvet box. "I'll put it back on you tonight, when we're home."

I snuggled into his side, silently thanking him for not asking why. I didn't need Tiffany judging my non-diamond or Mom and Dad trying to figure out what it meant. Manning was the one who always reminded me our relationship was nobody else's business. We were years beyond allowing anyone else to dictate how we should feel about each other.

He pushed the ring box back in his pocket and opened the front door for us.

"There you two are," Mom said as we walked back into the dining room. "We were about to give up and have some pie."

"We'll get it," Manning and I said at the same time.

We both laughed as Mom, Dad, and Tiffany stared blankly at us. Once, Manning and I had served my family pie together on special guest dishes. I'd snuck glances at him, trying to figure him out, and Manning was surely remembering the same thing.

I opened the Tupperware I'd brought as Manning uncovered the cake dish with Tiffany's pie. "Is this apple?" he asked. "Looks good."

I smiled sweetly at him. "I love you, Great Bear, but if you lay a finger on that pie, I'll toss that engagement ring in the garbage disposal and walk out of your life forever."

He guffawed a laugh, pushed aside the plate, and pulled me into his arms. "You didn't let me finish. I was saying that pie looks good for a second-rate pastry. You should know nothing, and nobody, could ever steal me away from my favorite flavor—blueberry."

BIG BEAR
SUMMER 2009

8

Despite a home filled with friends and family, I had no doubt who was tapping on my door at midnight. I turned on a lamp and got out of bed. With a knowing smile, I tied my robe around my waist.

I answered to find Manning leaning in the doorway, arms crossed over a black t-shirt. "Don't like knocking on my own bedroom door."

"You can't come in," I said.

"I'm not above begging." He looked me over. "Were you asleep?"

"Not even close."

"I didn't think so. Is it nerves?"

"No," I whispered, stepping into him. I'd slept without him enough nights while away at school, so now that I'd graduated and lived full time in Big Bear, I didn't want to sleep alone anymore. "I just want tomorrow to go well. Did you have a good time barbequing for everyone tonight?"

"Yeah. I don't know how much rehearsing we did, but it's nice to have us all in one place."

"Did you ever think, when you built this place, that the bedrooms would one day be filled with people we love?"

"Can't say that I did. I didn't think of myself as such a lucky bastard."

At tonight's rehearsal dinner, I'd looked around a backyard filled with people I cared about. As my eyes had landed on Manning at the grill, I'd wondered— could he say the same? Henry, Manning's only father figure, had made the trip with his entire family, and he'd brought Manning's aunt along as well. Gary was also in town with his wife, Lydia. The absence of Manning's parents and sister rarely affected us day to day, but this weekend, it would be unavoidable. Since it was my first time alone with him since that morning, I said, "I'm sorry your family couldn't be here."

He thumbed the hollow of my cheek. "My aunt came. Madison's always with me some way or another."

"But your parents—"

"Don't mean anything to me anymore."

I played with his shirt hem. "You were close with your mom before everything, though. I'm not saying she should've been here—I only wish things were different for you."

"And I'm saying that I don't wish a single thing was different."

I smiled, fisting his t-shirt to bring him closer. "You *are* a lucky bastard," I said, "just not tonight. I don't think we're supposed to be cavorting at all."

"Hmm." He sighed, rejected and dejected. "If only the wedding police weren't a real thing."

"Very funny," I said. "I'd like to take this moment to remind you that *you* were the one who wanted a 'traditional' wedding. I would've been fine keeping it low-key, but you had to have a blessing from my dad, a rehearsal dinner, a bouquet and boutonniere, Blue as a ring bearer—"

"I never said anything about spending a night apart, though."

"You don't get to pick and choose which traditions you abide by," I said, rising to the tips of my toes to kiss his cheek. "Enjoy a night to yourself in the guest room."

I went to shut the door when Manning caught it with his hand. "Aren't you the least bit curious as to why I'm here?"

"I know why you're here," I said, but the amused look on his face had me doubting myself.

"Give me some credit," he said. "I can go without it for an evening. I did it four nights a week for years."

"Not lately," I reminded him. "Ever since we finalized the wedding plans, it's as if you haven't been physically capable of keeping your hands to yourself."

"That's 'cause picturing you in a wedding dress drives me *insane*." He groaned, massaging the bridge of his nose, as if it actually pained him. "I can't talk about this or I'll break tradition and spoil our plans for tonight."

"*Plans*?" I asked, checking the clock on the nightstand. "It's after midnight on the day of our wedding."

He tugged on the sash of my robe. "Throw on some jeans and tennis shoes, and meet me out front."

"We can't go anywhere," I said. "We have a house full of guests."

"They won't even know we're gone. Come on. Hurry up."

"I'm the *bride*," I said. "I need my beauty rest."

He opened my robe. "You couldn't get any more beautiful."

The way his lids fell as he trailed a finger down the front of my nightie, I had a feeling if I didn't agree to go out, we'd wind up staying in and sacrificing sleep anyway.

"All right," I said, stopping his hand in its tracks. "You'd better head out front before we get ourselves in trouble."

Alone, I flipped on the closet light to change. Truthfully, I was grateful for whatever Manning had planned. Before he'd knocked, I'd been staring at the ceiling, overthinking what we were about to do. Marrying Manning wouldn't be hard—it was doing it in front of everybody we knew and loved that'd been keeping me up. My suggestion to go to City Hall had been genuine but *perhaps* one made out of fear. Up until January, he and I had lived in our own private bubble. We'd been spending time here and there with my family, but they'd only known as a couple seven months. It was as if we were all getting reacquainted.

As I left our bedroom and headed down a hallway of closed doors where my parents, Manning's aunt, and some of my girlfriends slept, I couldn't help worrying about standing up in front of all of them with a man no one thought I was supposed to end up with. Did they still have their doubts?

To Manning's credit, except for a libido in overdrive, he'd been nothing but calm about the wedding since he'd proposed. He had no doubts. No nerves. If anything, he'd been working harder than usual to ensure all the details were taken care of. So when I found him waiting at the base of the porch steps with Blue, looking every inch a man in jeans and fishing boots, the porch swing's floral printed cushions under one arm, any fears I had vanished. Tomorrow was about marrying the man I loved, a man both tough and sensitive, determined but attentive. It wasn't about anything or anyone else but us.

"Why are you wearing galoshes?" I asked, taking his outstretched hand. I started for his truck but he pulled me around the side of the house, toward the back. "And what're the cushions for?"

"Guess," he said.

Manning and I had explored the woods behind the house plenty of times. Usually we went back there for two reasons—to walk Blue, or to go on the lake. Neither of those seemed like great after-dark activities. "I'm stumped," I said.

As we crossed from our backyard into the woods, Manning kept me close with an arm around my shoulders. Blue darted through the trees but always sprinted back when we called for her. Perhaps if I'd been anywhere except the place I called home, I might've been spooked by the cover of darkness. By the rustling bushes, or the haunting hoots and flapping of wings echoing around us. Instead, I snuggled into the side of the man I knew would kill to protect me or die trying.

The closer we got to the edge of the forest, the more convinced I was that Manning had lost his mind and decided to recreate the night we'd snuck out of camp, gone for a drive, and wound up in the water.

The woods spit us out into a clearing that opened up to a tiny lake we'd come to know well. It was shallow, mostly off the map, and small enough for us to drift aimlessly. Manning kept the first dinghy he'd ever made there, tied to a stake in the ground. He'd built other boats—some he'd sold, and with help, a larger one we kept at one of Big Bear Lake's marinas—but we had this little slice of heaven all to ourselves most of the time.

"We're going on the lake?" I asked.

"Bingo," he replied. "Go on. Climb on over the starboard side." Manning winked before he added, "And into my lap." It was the same thing he'd said to me my first night at the house in Big Bear, and he knew I loved the word, pronounced star*bird*.

No matter how endearing his invitation, I stayed where I was. We'd made love in this boat. I'd laughed until my sides had ached watching Manning try and fail to catch a fish with his hands. We'd drifted around in it on hot afternoons eating orange slices as the sun had set. But we'd certainly never taken it out at night.

Blue whined, probably sensing she was about to get left behind. "Blue and I are going to need a bit of an explanation before we proceed," I said.

He squatted to untie the boat, and I heard the smile in his voice. "What's wrong? Don't trust me?"

"To steer this thing in the dark?"

"The stars are out." He gestured up at the sky. "They'll guide us, Birdy."

"Actually," I said, hands on my hips, "it's a crescent moon and particularly dark tonight."

"I know," he said. "I wish I could say I planned it that way, but we just got lucky."

Warily, I climbed over the starboard side and set up both cushions. Once I was seated at the bow, he pushed the boat through the weeds and waded in after it.

"Stay," he told Blue.

She barked once to get her point across but plopped down at the edge of the lake, watching us go as she had many times before.

"Where are we headed?" I asked once Manning had climbed in.

"To the middle." Slowly, he rowed us out on the water. As the night spread around us, complete stillness punctuated by occasional splashes and croaks, I began to wonder if the journey was the destination. Though Manning and I had planned a fairly low-key weekend for the wedding, there was no getting around the chaos that came with having friends and family in one place. Tiffany's dress had needed last minute altering. Henry's truck had broken down ten miles from the house. Our washing machine's hose had begun leaking hours before guests had arrived. It'd been days, maybe even weeks, since I'd experienced this kind of stillness and peace.

"Okay, this was a good idea," I admitted, shutting my eyes and relaxing against the back of the boat to enjoy the warm breeze.

"Yeah?" Manning asked. "How come?"

"It's so easy to get caught up in the details of making sure tomorrow goes smoothly. I want to look back and remember everything. It's good to slow down and take it all in." Smiling, I opened my eyes. "Feel free to remind me of that throughout the weekend."

"*Traditionally*," Manning said, "I'm not supposed to see you most of tomorrow, either. At least not until we've said 'I do.'"

I sighed. "I'm thinking I'll be doing away with some of these silly rituals at my next wedding."

"Your *next* wedding?" He dropped the paddles and stood, rocking the boat hard enough that I squealed and grabbed the sides. "Take that back."

"Or what?" I teased.

"I tip this boat over. It'd serve you right for antagonizing the bears."

In the dark, looming over me, he almost did look like a bear. "You wouldn't," I said.

"I might," he said, "if we weren't here."

"Where's here?"

"Middle of the lake. Best spot to see the show." He reached for me. "Come."

Taking his hand, I let him guide me forward to sit between his legs.

He enveloped me, hugging my back to his chest. "Look up."

I relaxed against him, resting my arms on his as I scanned the countless stars. In the pitch black, they shone especially bright. "They're beautiful," I said.

"You know I'll always move the stars for you if need be," he said. "Whatever it takes."

Though I appreciated the warmth behind his words, wasn't it possible some fates couldn't be rearranged? The vastness of the black sky and the sheer number of stars overhead made me feel small and insignificant—but not in a bad way. Did the universe have plans for us? Or had Manning and I really defined our own destiny? And what did either of those realities mean for our future?

It'd been many months since Manning and I had thrown out my birth control. Weeks since I'd had to stop making excuses not to get my wedding dress tailored. I supposed most women would've been happy not to walk down the aisle with a baby bump, but I'd almost planned on it. Manning wasn't worried. When it came up, he reminded me we had time. That it would happen. I wished I had the confidence he did, but I hadn't expected it to take this long.

Manning bent his mouth to my ear. "Lake?" he asked.

"Hmm?"

"Did you hear me?"

Whatever it takes. It occurred to me as we sat under the glittering stars that Manning would do anything in his power to move them in our favor—but what would it do to him if he couldn't?

"Is something wrong?" I asked.

"No. I just want you to know I don't take tomorrow lightly. My vows to love and care for you are a promise—always. No matter what comes our way."

"I know," I said.

"Open your hand."

I flipped my palm up, and he put something small and cool in it. I lifted it to my face. "I haven't seen this in months," I said, admiring the mood ring. "Where'd you find it?"

"In your jewelry box. I thought you might want it for tomorrow."

I slid it on, flexing my hand so we could both see it. "Madison would be standing up there with me if she were still alive," I said.

"I know." He held me a little more tightly, and we sat in silence until light streaked across the sky. "Look," I said, pointing. "A shooting star."

"Not quite," he said.

The timing was almost too perfect. As more silver stars sliced the blackness over our heads, I sat up straighter. This really *was* a show. "What's going on?" I asked.

"Moving stars."

I glanced over my shoulder at him. "What?"

"The Perseid meteor shower. Happens every August."

"The night before our wedding?" I asked.

"Technically, we're getting married *today*."

Hearing him say that, I got chills. By this time tomorrow night, Manning would be my husband. With happy tears in my eyes, I burrowed deeper into him as more and more meteors painted the sky. "Wait—is that why you insisted on this weekend when I suggested summer?" I asked.

He shrugged underneath me. "Once in a great while, we get the timing right."

"You're *such* a romantic."

"Only for you," he said, "but that's no surprise to anyone."

I twisted my head up to him. He kissed me slowly, deliberately, without spilling a drop of the overflowing love between us.

Above our heads, the sky moved and rearranged. It couldn't have been a more perfect way to start forever together. Perhaps our timing had always been right, and like Manning, I needed to let go and trust that in the end, we'd get everything we were supposed to.

9

"You aren't worried Manning will get cold feet?" Behind me, in my master bathroom, my sister wielded a curling iron in one hand and plucked at my hair with the other. "He could be halfway to Mexico by now. We'd have no idea until you were headed down the aisle."

"*Tiffany*," Mom scolded, glancing up from where she'd perched on the clawfoot tub. She held up her cell phone. "I just spoke to your father. He's with Manning, and everyone's accounted for."

I couldn't help but laugh as Val shook her head the same grave way she did whenever Hollywood announced another *Pirates of the Caribbean* movie. Halfway down the counter from us, in between applying fake lashes, she said, "*Lake* is more likely to bolt than Manning."

Tiffany paused in the middle of taking a break from curling my hair to touch up her own. She widened her eyes at me in the mirror. "Are you thinking about ditching him at the altar?"

"Of course not." Nothing could stop me from marrying the man of my dreams today. Still, the generally chilly idea of cold feet had me closing the lapels of my satin robe at the base of my throat. "This wedding is such a sure bet that if it doesn't happen, I'll move into your basement and do all your cooking and cleaning, like Cinderella."

"Really?" Tiffany asked, either missing the fact or not caring about my implication that she was an evil stepsister. She sighed happily as she swept my curls off my back to my shoulders. She looked over my head, studying her work in the mirror. "I mean, I'll have to check with Robby first. He's very particular about his space."

"Obviously," I agreed, exchanging a muted giggle with my mom. It wasn't that my joke was lost on Tiffany—she just always had Robby on the brain. I was glad for it. She'd been so distracted by him the past several months that she'd hardly paid Manning and me any attention. I'd met Doctor Robby with the nice, golden-blond hair to match his nice face. As my mom had promised, he was a stable and patient man who owned his home and was good with kids—at least, he usually had a lollipop on him. More importantly, he was as enamored by Tiffany's carefree approach to life as she was drawn to his adoration of her. Not long after Manning's and my visit in January, Robby had proposed.

And Tiffany never let us forget it.

"Ugh," she said. "My ring keeps getting caught in your hair."

"Which ring?" Val asked, rummaging through her makeup bag.

"My *engagement* ring," Tiffany said.

"Oh, right." Val popped open a blush compact, swiped a brush through it, and blew off the excess powder—all while managing a smirk. "I guess I forgot. Thanks for clarifying."

Tiffany shot Val a daggered look. How dare she forget such big news? I held in a laugh so I wouldn't further anger my sister. She was not only in charge of my wedding day hair, of which she currently had handfuls, but my makeup, too. I didn't want to walk down the aisle looking like a hairless blowup doll.

Once Val had finished applying her makeup, she disappeared and returned with her hands behind her back. "I finished your bouquet last night," she said. "I also tied together some lavender bunches for Tiffany, me, and the other bridesmaids to carry."

I tried to look around her. "Let me see."

She kept one hand behind her back as she passed me a blossoming bouquet of lilac, lavender, and greenery with cream and blush-colored roses. I inhaled the arrangement that complemented the plum color of their dresses. "I love it."

"And I made this," she said, placing a simple crown with the same flowers on my head. "Last night you said you needed something blue. I figured purple would work, but I added in some delphinium for good measure."

"Thank you," I said, hugging her.

Tiffany inspected the crown as well as the top of my head. "Do you even have anything borrowed?" she asked.

"No," I said, frowning. Manning had handled most of the small details for today. I'd been more concerned with making our houseguests comfortable and handling any last-minute arrangements.

"Your dress could be considered borrowed," Val suggested.

"True," Tiffany said. "It's looks like it's from the seventies. I don't know why you guys like that old stuff."

"And I don't know why you shop at Hollister when you're thirty-five," Val shot back.

"Girls," Mom said. "Try to remember it's Lake's day."

"I'd rather look too young than too old," Tiffany muttered as she gave Val's bridesmaid dress a disdainful onceover—even though it was the same one Tiffany wore. She slow-blinked at Val's Birkenstocks. "Are you a lesbian?"

"I don't identify with labels," Val said. "*Or* give life to stereotypes, unlike some people."

"So that's a yes. Are you in love with my sister?" Tiffany gasped. "Or with *me*?"

Val rolled her eyes and turned away, muttering, "I'm changing into heels before the ceremony."

No signature snippy comeback from Val? "Look, for the sake of getting through today," I said, "let's all agree to keep you two apart as much as possible. Tiffany has a very *contemporary* sense of style, and Val isn't in love with me or anyone else."

Val jerked her head over her shoulder, as if I'd surprised her, but her expression eased quickly. "It's almost time," she said, packing up her makeup bag. "Where are your boots?"

"Shoebox in my closet."

"I'll get them ready," she said on her way out.

Tiffany whipped a mascara wand from its tube like a sword from a sheath. She nodded at me. "Look at the ceiling."

As Tiffany attacked my bare lashes and my mother fluffed my generally unfluffable-able dress hanging on the back of the bathroom door, I wondered what was going on with Val. She wasn't a lesbian, even if she sometimes pretended to be to mess with people, but she *definitely* had a secret. She'd planned my bachelorette party, a trip to Napa Valley with our friends from each coast, and she'd been available to help with anything wedding-related—but I'd noticed her withdrawing from me the past year. I'd thought maybe I'd been ignoring her too much for Manning, but when I'd asked to come spend a weekend at her house in Los Angeles recently, she'd made up some excuse about getting it fumigated. Val could charm and convince and deflect like a pro, but when it came to the people she cared about, she was a shit liar. In the flurry of wedding activity, I hadn't had a chance to get to the bottom of her behavior, though.

"I'll make sure everyone's getting seated," Mom said, leaving me alone with Tiffany.

And her boobs.

They nearly spilled out of her strapless dress and into my lap as she put the final touches on my makeup. Most likely, she'd picked a size smaller than she needed. "I think you hurt Val's feelings," I said.

"She doesn't have any," Tiffany replied. "Part your lips."

I slackened my jaw as she finished off my makeup with a pale pink gloss. She stepped aside to give me the mirror. For all her extravagance, she'd always been good at keeping my look natural. I angled my head, rounding my cheeks as they glowed and shimmered.

Tiffany held out a hand mirror. "For the back."

I stood and turned. Topped by Val's crown of flowers, my hair fell—nay, *cascaded*—in long loose curls. "You should've been a cosmetologist, Tiff."

"I know." She circled me as if I were a science project. "I'm so glad you let your hair grow out a little. Anything above the shoulders doesn't suit you."

She cocked her head. "But I think you need more makeup for pictures."

Whenever I dressed up for a night out with Manning, he'd treat me like a princess—but once we got home and he unhooked my jewelry, slid off my heels, unzipped my dress, and unpinned my hair, I became a goddess under his worship. For him, less would always be more. "It's perfect," I said.

"Fine, but come see me between the ceremony and pictures for a touch-up. And *try* not to cry."

I turned to my sister. She'd pulled her hair back into a chignon, and her icy blue eyes warmed against shimmery skin and long, jet-black lashes. She looked different—from me and from herself. Today of all days, there was a stillness in her I'd rarely seen. It made little sense considering she'd have every reason to be upset, or to have blown off the wedding entirely. I grabbed her for a hug. "Thank you," I said.

It took her a moment, but she patted me on the back. "Okay, okay. I can't have my sister looking sloppy on her wedding day."

"I meant thank you *for being here*," I said with a laugh as I pulled back to look her in the face. "Are you okay with all of this, or are you pretending?"

She blinked at me. "You've *seen* me and Robby together, right? He loves me so much that the little stuff doesn't matter anymore." She rolled her eyes. "Not that your wedding is little—geez. Sorry. Robby says people are intimidated by me, and I should be more careful with my words."

117

Oh, my sister. She hadn't changed, but she was trying—I supposed I had to give her some credit for that. At this point, aside from developing a little empathy, I wasn't sure I even wanted her to change that much. When she was no longer a threat to me, her behavior was kind of entertaining. "I'm not intimidated by you," I said, "but I used to be."

"Really? I could see that. Big sister and all." She grinned. "Anyway, I'm not sure I'd be here today if I hadn't met Robby, but I did, so I'm glad I came."

"I would've understood if you hadn't, but honestly, something huge would've been missing without you here."

"Do you really feel that way?" she asked.

The idea of Tiffany staying home and angry this weekend gave me no pleasure. I'd only ever wanted her to succeed by following her own path—I'd just wished that path had been heading in the opposite direction of Manning. I nodded, smiling. "Yes. I'm sorry for everything, but I hope we can both recognize it worked out for the best."

"It did." She wet the tip of her thumb and smeared away something on my cheek. "Manning deserves to be happy, and I realize now that he never was. I talked to him for a while last night—he's a different man."

Tiffany knew Manning in ways I didn't. She'd been with him day in and day out when he'd suffered over me and struggled with his demons. I knew he was happy, but hearing Tiffany say it, my throat thickened. "I could barely comprehend what love was at sixteen, and I know you didn't believe me back then, but I felt it for him."

"Oh, geez. I told you not to cry." Tiffany twisted around to swipe a tissue from the bathroom counter. As she did, I noticed her zipper stretching at the seams. She turned back with tears in her eyes—and *that* was the giveaway. Tiffany didn't waste good makeup on crying. "Tiff?" I asked.

She dabbed at the corner of my eye. "What?"

Could that stillness in her be a result of something greater than her love for Robby? "Did you pick a date yet?"

"No." Her cheeks tinged the slightest shade of pink. "I know we told you guys fall, but fall is so predictable. We're going to wait until next year."

"I see."

Her chest rose and fell with each breath. Now that I'd noticed that her dress was tight, her breasts almost seemed to grow before my eyes.

"Is there another reason you're waiting?" I asked.

She balled up the tissue, shifting her eyes to meet mine. "What kind of reason?"

"Maybe that you don't want to order a dress in a bigger size?"

She narrowed her eyes, and for a second, I worried I'd gotten it wrong. Thinking she might be pregnant, I'd just implied my sister was gaining weight, which would be a surefire way to undo all the progress we'd made recently. But then, she shrugged.

"Maybe. But today is *your* day," she said. "It's your wedding. Don't worry about me."

Today was *my* day? Now I knew there was something fundamentally different about her. She was giving me the spotlight, possibly for the first time ever. Either she'd been abducted by aliens and they'd sent down a nicer version of her, or her hormones were going haywire and the pregnancy had softened her. I'd heard of that happening—then again, I'd also heard of Roswell. "You *are* pregnant." I tried to contain my smile. "Were you planning it?"

"*I* wasn't. Robby probably poked holes in the condom."

With no response to that, I laughed nervously. "Does Mom know?"

"No. I'm not that far along, so I don't want to say anything." She glanced over her shoulder. "Considering what happened before, I'm scared to even let myself think it's true."

I nodded. I got anxious when my period was even a day late, so I understood. I promised myself this time, no matter what, I'd be there for Tiffany. There'd be no keeping my distance like before when she'd needed family by her side. "Between us, Manning and I have been trying."

"I'm not surprised." She squeezed my arm. "We can be pregnant together."

As soon as excitement buzzed through me, it fizzled. Manning and I had been off birth control long enough for me to understand I didn't have any say over the timing. "It's been a while," I said. "I actually thought I might be waddling down the aisle."

"How long?" she asked.

"Almost a year. But that's including the time it takes for birth control to wear off."

"Oh." She nodded a little, blinking away. "That's not that long. And on the bright side, you're *not* waddling. That would be a terrible look on your wedding day."

I wasn't sure I agreed. I remembered how the thought of me as a pregnant bride had driven Manning wild. "You're probably right."

My mom returned and took my dress off the back of the door. "They're about ready for us."

I glanced at her in the mirror. "I need help getting into that."

"Go to the bathroom first," Mom and Tiffany said at the same time.

"I don't have to."

"Make yourself," Tiffany said.

"You can do it," Mom added.

"O-*kay*," I said, mostly out of a fear they wouldn't let me leave otherwise.

When I'd finished, I found my mom, Tiffany, and Val in the bedroom, all holding open the gown.

"I think it should go over her head," Val was saying.

"After I just spent an hour on her hair and makeup?" Tiffany asked. "She can step into it."

"The top part is too tight," Val said. "It won't fit over her hips—no offense, Lake. It's not you, it's the dress. I do this all the time on set."

"Whatever," Tiffany said. "If she gets foundation on it, that's on you."

Oddly, their bickering made me smile. It was normal, and normal was good today. I didn't want anything more than to walk down the aisle, marry my love, and eat and drink with friends and family. I slid off my robe and raised my arms as they worked on the sleeves and guided my head through the neckline.

Once my mom had zipped me up and arranged the dress how she wanted, she guided me over to the floor-length mirror to help me into my shoes. I'd picked up my off-the-shoulder, long-sleeved cream dress from a secondhand store in town. The lace bodice managed to hug my breasts without cutting off my air, and the skirt fell in a loose column. It'd been Tiffany's uncharacteristic suggestion to have fun with the shoes, so Val had helped me pick out chestnut-brown leather booties to fit the outdoor setting of our ceremony and reception.

I turned to the side, checking myself from all angles. The long lace sleeves bared only my shoulders. The toes of my booties stuck out from under the hem. I wasn't the most stylish, most glamorous, or the sexiest bride in the world, but I looked like myself—a woman about to walk down the aisle to the man she loved. Luckily, Manning made me feel sexy no matter what I wore. Still, I smiled to myself knowing I had some special wedding lingerie for him later.

As I started to turn away from the mirror, my gaze snagged on my right hand. The deep purple color of the mood ring Manning had slid onto my finger in the boat was vibrant against the cream lace. It had turned that color the night I'd found my way back to Manning in Big Bear, after we'd eaten and argued and cried and made love—and I wasn't sure it'd changed since. That purple was our shade of happiness and the reason I'd chosen a plum color scheme for the wedding. Manning giving it to me on the lake the night before was no coincidence. I did have something borrowed after all. I considered it Madison's ring first, and a symbol of her presence.

I flexed my hand against the dress one last time, then turned back to Mom, Tiffany, and Val. "I'm ready."

————

On a warm summer evening, I stood on my back porch overlooking friends and family as I prepared to marry my best friend. A violinist played over the murmurs of the crowd, the sun orange as it began to lower behind the mountains and trees. Manning and his friends had organized our backyard with wooden folding chairs divided by an aisle lined with lit lanterns.

Of my five bridesmaids, one was from Pomona, and the other two had driven in from Los Angeles.

The audience had seemingly arranged itself—friends from New York took up one row, while other sections had been taken over by Californians, grad school classmates, or locals Manning and I had befriended. Tiffany blew Robby a kiss from her bridesmaid post. Val's normally wry expression warmed and softened as she winked at someone in the second row. That *someone* had golden hair that was now down to his broad, suited surfer's shoulders. Corbin had narrowly missed my forcing him to be a bridesmaid.

Opposite of my friends and sister stood Henry, Gary, and a few men in the construction business Manning had become close with since moving to Big Bear.

The bridal party flanked a wedding arch I'd never seen. Crafted of the same honey wood in the house and adorned with cream gauze, ivy, pinecones, and white twinkle lights, I understood why I'd known nothing about it. It had to be a wedding gift to me from Manning. At the foot of one side of the arch, Blue wore a harness with a pouch for her role as ring bearer.

I looked everywhere but at Manning. Once I did, that would be it for me. I'd never been the same girl after Manning and I had met eyes on the street all those years ago, and I wouldn't be the same woman once I saw him waiting on his bride.

With his thoughtfulness filling my heart, I descended the porch to meet my dad at the base of the steps. He offered me his elbow. "You look like one of those princesses in the fairytales you watched as a young girl."

I smiled. "All Tiffany's doing."

"I have no doubt." We looped arms, and he guided me toward the aisle. "Are you nervous?"

"No," I answered and finally met Manning's gaze. Undoubtedly, his eyes had been on me the whole time. Everything else fell away, my nose tingling. With a cream rose pinned to his suit lapel to match my bouquet, he adjusted the knot of his black tie and watched my every move with melted-chocolate brown eyes. I wanted to smile at him. To thank him for the love and mastery it'd surely taken to design the back lawn into a rustic paradise—from the arch to the twinkle lights strung in the trees, over chairs, and hanging from the trellis, to the picnic tables he'd rented so we could host the reception here. I wanted to blow him a kiss, call for him, cry tears of joy. But I couldn't do any of that. Both Manning and I seemed frozen in the moment, just our hearts beating—syncing, as I was certain I actually *felt* his—and the tether between us pulling me closer and closer to him.

If there were any other eyes on me besides Manning's as I walked down the aisle, I didn't notice. I heard only what I felt—pine needles crunching underfoot, the brush of my dad's suit against my dress, and the echo of my heartbeat in my ears. The setting sun cast a glow on Manning as we reached him.

My dad turned to me. "Love you, Lake," he said, and that was enough, but he added, "I'm proud of the woman you've become, even if I had little hand in it."

"You were there with me every day, Dad, even if we were apart." The back of my throat burned as I held back tears. I hugged him. "For better or worse."

He chuckled, then let me go before nodding at Manning. I stepped up to the altar, pausing to run my fingertips over the smooth wood. Carved into the underside of the arch, where only Manning, the minister, and I could see, were tiny, almost invisible stars, and the initials *L+M* in the center.

"Charles helped," Manning said.

My dad smiled at me as he took his seat. I moved in front of Manning with tears in my eyes, but I could hardly look at him without losing it. I scratched Blue's head, then glanced at the ground in a vain attempt to compose myself . . . and noticed Manning's shoes. At my urging, he'd spent time and money getting a custom suit for today, but I'd forgotten to ask about his footwear. Through my teary vision, I inhaled a laugh at his Timberlands.

"Friends and family—" the officiant began, pausing as Manning put a knuckle under my chin to lift my eyes to meet his. I swallowed thickly but held his gaze and heard nothing else until it was my turn to repeat my vows, and then Manning his.

I'd asked Manning once, months ago, if we should write our own vows, but he'd said no. He wanted to marry me in front of friends and family, but our most private and intimate feelings were just that—private and intimate. After so many years of not sharing with Manning how I felt, he was the only person I cared to tell anyway.

We exchanged rings. Manning placed my palm in his and kissed the back of it before sliding on a simple gold band. I put a matching ring on his roughened hand.

"By the power vested in me," the minister said, "I now pronounce you husband and wife. Manning—"

Manning's mouth slid into a sly smile. "Yes?"

"You may now kiss your bride."

Manning gathered me in his arms, but instead of kissing me, he shifted to whisper in my ear. "I love you, *Lake Sutter.* I don't know why you trusted me that first day or any day after it. You mesmerized me. There was, and still is, something in the way you are. Your blue eyes brought peace and light to my dark and noisy head." He drew back and took a moment to collect himself. "I think maybe you saved me, Birdy."

With his last words, my tears finally slid free. I shook my head. "You saved yourself."

"*You* did. More than once. If my life wasn't everything it is," he said, nodding over the crowd toward our house, "it would be nothing."

I fisted his lapels to pull him closer, crying openly now. "Manning."

"Yeah, Birdy."

He picked me up by my waist so I could whisper in his ear. "I told you City Hall would've been fine, that the where and how and when didn't matter. But you saw right through me. Deep down, I still held on to the fear that we wouldn't make it here. That we wouldn't get this moment. So, I pretended it wasn't important who witnessed it, or how it was done, but it is, and you knew that. Maybe I saved your life, I don't know about that, but you love me with an intensity that can't be reckoned with. I fear for anyone who tries to get in our way. I'd say I want to spend forever with you, but forever isn't long enough."

"No, it isn't," he agreed.

"Now kiss me, Great Bear, and let's make this official."

10

Two hours into our marriage, I'd already lost my husband. *Husband.* My toes curled, and not just because I was failing to contain my happiness. The word *husband* actually did things to me—things that made me want to steal him away from the reception. That might've been possible anywhere else, but not in our home, where guests would easily miss us.

My gut told me he'd snuck off on purpose, so I wasn't surprised to find him in the front yard with Henry and my dad. Each of them stood with loosened ties, a tumbler in one hand, and a cigar in the other.

"What'd I tell you, Manning?" Dad asked, winking at me as I picked up the skirt of my dress and descended the porch steps. "Now that you're married, you won't get ten minutes to yourself."

"That so?" Manning opened an arm to me, and I fit myself to his side.

"I don't think he minds," Henry said with a gentle smile.

"I'm not here to force him back to the party," I promised, sliding one arm inside his suit jacket and around his waist. "I just missed him."

Manning set his drink on the porch railing and balanced the cigar next to it. I lifted my face when he cupped my cheek for a kiss. "I keep meaning to tell you how beautiful you look," he said.

"You told me," I said. "About ten times so far. The last time was thirty minutes ago."

"Well, I've been meaning to say it for thirty minutes."

I could've basked in his adoration all night, and I planned to, but that would have to wait.

"I recognize that look," Dad said, sounding as if he might be approaching his drink limit. "You two better be careful."

Manning pecked my forehead, then took his cigar from the railing. "Why's that?"

I had a good buzz going from the champagne, so I picked up Manning's drink. "What is this?" I asked, sniffing it.

"Scotch," Manning answered as I took a sip. "It's strong."

Dad blew out a cloud of white smoke, then waved it away. "Kaplan women get pregnant at the drop of a hat."

I spit out the Scotch and coughed so hard that Manning took the drink away.

"Easy," Dad said. "That's three-hundred-dollar liquor, Lake."

Manning patted my back. "You all right?" he asked.

Eyes watering, I nodded. Then I shook my head. *No.* Had my father really said that? My dad didn't bother with things that didn't interest him. If he took to meddling in my sex life the way he had my education, then I was definitely *not* all right.

"I'll get you some water," Henry said, setting down his cigar to go in the house.

My burning throat kept me from thanking him— and from stopping my dad from making his point, which he always did.

"When your mother told me she wanted a kid," Dad said, "I wasn't sure we were ready. Well, damn if we didn't conceive Tiffany the moment I agreed. Sure felt that way."

"*Dad,*" I protested, my voice creaking. "Overshare."

"It's basic biology, Lake. It was the same with you." He turned to Manning. "I told Cathy we ought to give Tiffany a sibling, and nine months later, she had one."

I hid my face in Manning's jacket. "Make it stop."

Manning chuckled. "It's come up a few times, sir."

"That's what I was worried about," Dad said. "Keep in mind that Lake has a lot ahead of her. Just because she's done with school doesn't mean this next part is easy."

Henry appeared next to me with a water. "Don't want grandkids?" he asked my dad.

I took the bottle with a "thank you" and gulped water through my embarrassment.

"I do, and Lord knows Cathy does, but there's a time for that, and it isn't when she owes tens of thousands in student loans."

"Students loans are an epidemic in this country," Manning agreed.

Since Manning was always reminding me when I stressed about money that my loans were the good kind of debt, I knew they didn't bother him; this was his way of changing the subject. Certainly my dad's words needled him the way they did me. But then, their meaning started to settle in—and a far bigger, more disheartening realization eclipsed any of my irritation. Kaplan women *were* actually extremely fertile. In fact, Tiffany had ruined my first shot at a relationship with Manning years ago with her sudden pregnancy. And this time, she hadn't even been *trying* with Robby.

Kaplan women get pregnant at the drop of a hat.

Each month I got my period, Manning reassured me it was nothing to worry about. These things took time—they happened on their own schedule. Though pregnancy had definitely been on my mind,

132

Manning's Zen attitude, and the fact that we'd started a little earlier than we'd planned, hadn't given me a strong sense of urgency. But now, hours into our marriage, I worried about what lay ahead—and behind us. Tonight, Manning had made me his wife. Beginning with our week in New York, we'd had plenty of conversations over the years about children. I wanted a family, but Manning *needed* one. A little girl to protect, to right the wrongs of his past and his father. Or a son to spend weekends with, fishing on the lake or building furniture in the work shed. I'd just stood in front of our friends and family and promised Manning a future, a family, a forever. Pressure built each month I got my period, and I'd definitely considered that there might be an issue, but for the first time I wondered—was there a chance I physically couldn't get pregnant?

Ever?

"Feel better?" Henry asked.

I blinked out of my daze. "Sorry?"

"The coughing. Went down the wrong tube, eh?"

"Yes. Thank you for the water." I cleared my throat. "I haven't had a chance to meet your granddaughter yet. She's barely made a peep all night."

"Kara was so worried the baby would ruin the ceremony. She stood in the back with her the whole time in case they needed to make a break for it."

"How old?" Dad asked.

Henry smiled through a puff of his cigar. "Five months. My first grandkid."

Manning shook his head, lifting his glass. "She's beautiful. I feel like an uncle."

"You are, kid. We're lucky that Kara and her husband moved down the street. I see Abby almost every day."

"You might not feel so lucky when they're calling you to babysit every weekend," Dad said.

"I don't mind." Henry swirled his drink. "I'm retired. I could use the money."

My dad looked disgusted. "They *pay* you?"

Henry laughed, and it was such a rare, joyous sound that I joined in. "I'm kidding," he said. "I got the time, and the baby grows on you."

"Grows on you? You're *crazy* for her." Manning got an ashtray from the deck and put out his cigar. "You're like a new man, Henry."

"A baby'll do that to you."

"I look forward to it." Manning set down his drink and my empty water bottle before taking my hand. "Come on and I'll introduce you."

I flashed a wave at my dad and Henry as Manning led me around the side of the house. So I'd stolen him away after all—which reminded me why I'd gone looking for him in the first place.

I stopped walking when we were halfway around the house and pulled Manning back by his hand.

"What is it?" he asked, turning to me.

"There's something about the word *husband*, isn't there?" I asked. "Try it."

He stepped into me, lowering his voice as he emphasized, "*Husband*."

I laughed. "I mean try it the other way. Call me your wife."

"My wife." With his next step, we retreated until my back was up against the side of the house and we were hidden from the partygoers. "I really fucking like it, *Wife*."

From the backyard, I recognized the thumping bass of an Usher song on the sound system we'd rented. Perfect baby-making music. I slid my hands up Manning's suit and around his neck. "Me too."

He took my face in his hands and, for the first time as my husband, kissed me for real—without eyes on us and less politely than he had in front of others. "We can't do this now," he said. "I mean, *I* can do this now . . ." He moved his pelvis against my stomach, pinning me to the wall with his growing hard-on. "But I love your dress too much to risk ruining it."

"*That's* your concern? My dress?" I breathed. "Not the guests a few feet away?"

He half-smiled. "Them too. I want to preserve this dress, but once it comes off . . ."

I bit my bottom lip. "What happens then?"

"I'm taking full advantage of our first night as a married couple. No distractions."

Not that Manning was ever really distracted when it came to sex, but tonight, the determination in his expression made me wriggle between his body and the wall. "I can't wait."

"Stop drinking," he said. "I've only had two tonight. I recommend you get a coffee and take it easy. Conserve your energy."

I frowned. "How come?"

"We're going to be at it all night."

"Manning." I blushed at his unapologetic bluntness. "We have people staying at the house until tomorrow."

"Not anymore. I booked them all at a hotel in town."

I put my hands on his chest, trying to read him in the dark. "No you didn't."

"I did. I'm sorry, Lake." He shrugged. "I tried to tell you I wouldn't have people in my home on my wedding night."

"And I told you I'd be quiet."

He snorted. "Impossible. Not in our bed, not the first night you're my wife. I would've had to take you out to the stable."

I scoff-laughed, shoving him away. "I'm not a wild animal," I said, walking off.

He grabbed my hand and fell in step beside me. "But *I* am, and you're in heat, so you better gird your loins."

"Gird my loins?" I asked. "I'm *in heat*?"

"Maybe. You're about halfway between periods, right?"

I stopped and turned to him, taking my hand back. "Wait, what?" I asked. "You're serious?"

"I don't know for sure," he said. "But this is around the time you'd be ovulating."

"You think about that?" I asked.

"Not a lot," he said, laughing, "but sometimes. I was paging through some of your textbooks a while back and got curious about the process."

I put my hands on my hips. "But is that something you plan sex around?"

"I don't, not that I'd need to." He closed the distance between us, tucking my hair behind my ear. "You initiate more around this time each month. You never noticed?"

"No," I said. "I mean, of course I understand how it works given what I do, but I wasn't keeping track or anything."

"It's not a big deal," he said. "You know I'm ready to go any time, any day, ovulating or not. But sometimes I wonder . . . and I can tell you I'll be wondering tonight if . . ."

"If what?"

"If we're conceiving."

"*That's* what you're thinking about during sex?"

He lowered his head—and his voice. "Whether I'm putting a baby in you? Yeah, sometimes, and it gets me so fucking hot, Lake."

"Okay, okay," I said, my face warming as I put my hands on his chest to hold him off. The hunger developing in his eyes told me we were a few moments away from me having to walk into the party ahead of him to shield his crotch. "Let's pick this up later when we can do something about it."

"Sooner the better," he growled in my ear, as if it were some kind of threat.

I shivered, and he slid an arm around my shoulders on our way back to the reception. Anything to do with providing, protecting, or mating, and Manning turned into a caveman. I loved how turned on it made him, but it also shone light on a truth I wasn't sure I was ready to face—Manning would not accept anything less than a biological baby. What if I couldn't give him that? What if I couldn't give *myself* that? I wanted to raise Manning's boy into the man his father was, or teach my little girl that she deserved to be treated with all the love and respect her father gave her.

As we rounded the side of the house, we were met with a chorus of suggestive *oohs* and *aahs* that made me blush. Normally, presumptions or interest in our sex life from anyone would bother Manning, but he just rolled his eyes and hugged me closer. He'd been in great spirits all weekend. I had to shake this feeling of *what if*, or I was going to cast a storm cloud over one of the best days of my life.

Kara, Henry's daughter, stood near a picnic table swinging her newborn side to side in rhythm with the

Black Eyed Peas. Her hair was coming loose from its bun, brown strands framing her face. Blue lay at her feet, her ears up as she watched the crowd.

"Lake wanted to meet the baby," Manning said to Kara as we approached.

Kara smiled. "She's asleep now, but it's okay. She's cuter that way."

I peered at the rosy-cheeked little girl. "I'm glad you and your husband could make it," I told Kara.

"Us too. I'd wake her up for you, but she'd make a scene. I haven't stopped rocking her since we got out of the car."

"Did you get to eat at least?" I asked.

"A few bites here and there."

"We'll have to get you some food." I squatted to pet Blue. "I hope the dog wasn't bothering you."

"Not at all. She's playing lookout." Kara bounced as she spoke, pausing to blow a piece of hair out of her eyes. "Our dog does the same thing. When there are people around, she stands near the baby."

"What kind of dog?" I asked.

"Lab mix. We got her from the pound a few years ago and weren't sure how she'd do with a baby, but she's been very protective."

"They're great with kids. I help our local shelter place animals, and Labs are always the first request by young families."

Kara stretched her neck. "They're easy, and that's the best you can hope for with a newborn in the house."

"Why don't you let me take over," Manning suggested to Kara, gesturing for the baby. "You look exhausted. Take a break."

Her mouth dropped open. "Are you sure? It's not as easy as it looks, trying to keep her moving without waking her."

I stood, smoothing out my dress. "He'll be fine. I can take you to get some food."

"You two are angels," Kara whispered, stealthily passing Abby to Manning. The newborn looked even smaller and paler in his arms, her pink bow and smooth skin soft against his bronzed forearms. "Thank you."

He hardly looked up from the little girl as he murmured, "No problem."

It was possible that the last baby Manning had held was Madison, yet he cradled Kara's daughter with ease, swaying her side to side. He seemed to have forgotten we were even standing there, completely enamored by a little girl that wasn't even his own. Kara's daughter was precious, but I doubted I'd feel that same connection Manning obviously did unless she was mine. Then again, I'd never met anyone who loved as deeply as he did. Maybe Manning was enjoying himself, but I had no doubt he'd be forever changed holding his own child.

As I was about to turn away, Manning glanced up at me. I read what he didn't say clearly in his eyes. *I want one.*

I quickly switched my attention to Kara. "Let's eat," I said to her.

Manning had wanted to work the grill tonight—probably because it would've gotten him out of socializing—but with over fifty guests, I'd convinced him to hire a local barbeque restaurant to cater. I took Kara to a buffet table of warming dishes, salad, and a meat station managed by the head chef.

"Thank you so much for the invitation to stay with you," she said as I handed her a plastic plate. "We would've, but with the baby, it was easier to get a hotel."

"I understand. I figured with a newborn it might help if we offered."

"We appreciated it." She served herself salad and passed me the tongs. "The ceremony was beautiful. Manning looked so happy during your first dance. He must really love you. Or Aerosmith."

I snorted. We'd slow-danced to "Crazy," possibly the worst wedding song in history, but Manning had wanted it. It'd been playing on our bus ride to camp in 1993, and Manning had later told me it was one of the first moments he'd realized how deep into trouble he was getting with me. Mostly because as a man normally in control, he couldn't get himself *out* of trouble.

"Manning's been happy in general lately," I said. "I know he's glad you and your dad could be here."

"They have a great relationship. I think my dad would've loved to have him as a son-in-law if I'd been older when Manning had started coming around." As we worked our way toward the meat station, she elbowed me. "Good thing I was only seven."

Kara had a warm, nonjudgmental smile; the kind that put me instinctively at ease. "I met Manning when I was sixteen," I confessed. I hadn't said that to many people, and certainly not those I barely knew. Manning and I were married now, and while our age difference had once seemed like the world, it was now an anecdote of a hard-earned history nobody could take from us. "He wouldn't touch me, but that only made me want him more."

"I understand completely. I wasn't going to say, but I definitely had a small crush on him from about ten to seventeen." She giggled. "He was so handsome and mature and *serious*. Nothing like the boys I went to school with."

"So serious," I agreed. It made me laugh now to think of how tense Manning must've been when I was around back then. "How'd you meet your husband?"

"Work." She shrugged, spooning mashed potatoes onto her plate. "Not nearly as exciting as stealing my sister's ex-con husband."

I laughed too hard at that. "*Exciting* is one way of putting it."

I introduced Kara to the restaurant's head chef, and he sliced us some steak and pork. The moment she and I stopped talking, I could almost feel Manning's adoration radiating from thirty feet away. Part of me wanted to look back and glean some hope from the sight of him with Abby, and the other part worried it'd be an image that would haunt me more and more with each month my period returned. "What's it like having a newborn in the house?" I asked Kara, both out of curiosity and to distract myself.

"It's . . ." She half-laughed. "It's as amazing as everyone says, and about as awful as nobody says. Everything you hear about—lack of sleep, shit everywhere, tension in your marriage—times it by ten."

"It sounds like more of an adventure than anything."

"It so is. Magical, too. *That* part you can't really describe." At the end of the buffet, we each picked a fork and knife from a pile of silverware. "What about you and Manning?" she asked. "I mean, not to add pressure. I know how annoying it is to get those questions, especially on your wedding day."

Maybe it wasn't just that Kara had an open, trustworthy face, but also that she was one of the few people in attendance who'd shown up for Manning. She'd known him before I had, and she cared about him. "Between you and me," I said, "Manning and I are trying. It's soon, but sometimes it feels like we waited our whole lives to get to this day. Life is short. We shouldn't have to wait for the things we want anymore."

"That's so romantic," she said, sighing. We set our plates and silverware on a high-top table to eat. "I can't get over the way he looks at you. It's every girl's dream." She forked some spinach leaves and grimaced. "I hope I didn't scare you off the baby thing."

"No," I said. "I mean, I don't know if we really grasp what we're getting ourselves into. Admittedly, we didn't think it through very hard. I only graduated a few months ago, and I'm about to start work . . ."

"Yeah, but there's never really a good time, you know?" She nodded behind me. "I mean, seems like Manning might be thinking it through pretty hard right now."

Thinking it through? As much as I hated to admit it, my dad's words earlier made sense. Now wasn't the best time for a baby. Was Manning having second thoughts, too? I turned, expecting to see Abby bawling in his arms and exasperation on his face. Instead, she slept soundly. His eyes were still glued to her as he held her against his chest.

I'd never seen Manning so gentle. So lost. He rarely let his guard down in public or took his eyes off what was happening around him—a side effect of his time in jail. He was a natural at this, probably more so than I would be. Then again, he'd done it before. He'd been old enough when his sister was born to help raise her.

"I think it's safe to say he wants one," Kara added.

A lump formed in my throat. "He does."

11

Kara and I were still standing at a high-top table with our half-finished dinners, watching Manning with her baby, when Val strode over waving a plastic champagne flute at us.

"Who are we gossiping about?" she asked, then gasped as her eyes landed on Manning. "*Look* at him. He's in heaven."

"All right," I said, turning forward again. I could've stood and stared at him the rest of the night, memorizing every breath he held, the way he hunched over the baby, warning others off. That was why I had to look away. "Let's not make a spectacle of him."

"Oh my God," my mom squealed behind me. "Lake, are you seeing this?"

"I saw, Mom," I said as she walked up. I checked

over my shoulder, but Manning still hadn't noticed he was drawing an audience. "Leave him alone or you might spook him."

"He's just so sweet." She nudged me. "Meant to have a baby of his own in his arms."

I turned to Val. She was an easy target, and it probably wasn't fair to take aim, but I'd need big guns to get us off this subject. "You've been avoiding me lately. Why?"

My plan worked. Mom and Kara looked back at Val.

"*What?*" she asked. "How can I be avoiding you while standing in front of you?"

"Normally, you're up my butt about everything from my relationship to my job to what I ate for dinner. Lately, you've been quiet on all fronts."

"What's left to say?" she asked, motioning around the yard. "You have it all figured out."

"I don't buy it. Where there's no drama, you'll invent it. You do that for a living." Val was always working on some kind of script. She'd recently directed her third short film and it'd been picked up by a couple smaller festivals. I narrowed my eyes at her. "It has to be a guy. You're seeing someone, and you don't want me to know about it."

She wagged her champagne at me. "It could be a woman, according to your sister."

"Don't change the subject."

"Leave her alone, honey," Mom said. "Maybe it's an ex and they want some privacy."

"Julian?" I asked myself, shaking my head. "No. Not unless you had a lobotomy. Although, if he moved back from Peru or wherever—"

"Portugal, and no, it's not him." Val tugged up her strapless dress as it sagged. "It's not anyone."

"It's not?" I asked. "Swear on Gus Van Sant?"

"Do you even know who he is?"

"One of the directors you always talk about."

"Don't make me swear on genius filmmakers." She sighed. "I don't want to talk about this tonight."

I got the acute feeling we were being watched, so I looked over Val's shoulder. Ten feet away, Corbin ate cake, pretending not to listen. "Why are you spying?" I asked him.

Val looked over her shoulder, and muttered what sounded like "fuck" before she tipped back her head and finished off her champagne.

"I wasn't," he said, swaggering over in his normal Corbin way—confident but humble, a combination only he could pull off. "Just trying to enjoy my cake."

Val's jaw dropped. "How many slices have you had?"

"Only three."

"You had a bag of M&M's on the way over here."

He raised his arms in exasperation. "Who are you, the dessert police?"

She laughed, shoving his arm. "If you think you'll be tall and skinny forever, you're in for a rude surprise."

Their easy banter wasn't unusual, but what tipped me off was the way Val blushed at Corbin's flirtatious smile.

"You guys drove up here together?" I asked.

Her mirth vanished as if she'd just remembered I was standing there. "It made the most sense," she said—or more like *recited*. "We both live in L.A., so Corbin picked me up on the way from Malibu. It really would've been silly to drive separately. With gas prices what they are these days—"

"Take it down a notch," Corbin said out of the side of his mouth. "Overboard."

I narrowed my eyes at them, recalling the way her expression had softened while smiling at Corbin during the ceremony. "Are you two sleeping together?"

"*Lake*," Mom scolded.

"Are we—*what*?" Val scoffed. "Me? And Corbin? Who said that—what makes you think . . .?"

Though her squirming was a thing to see, and almost too good to put a stop to, I deadpanned, "Call it a hunch."

Her entire face reddened and Corbin looked at the ground as we waited. Even Kara leaned in, seemingly interested in the answer.

"Corbin," I said. He glanced up. I'd had a few minutes here and there with him throughout the night, but ever the gentleman, Corbin kept excusing himself to give other people more time with me. "What are you hiding from me? And you have frosting on your face."

He wiped his mouth with the back of one hand as he threw his other arm around me. "I'm hiding lots from you."

I elbowed him in the ribs, and he winced. "Christ, Kaplan. I fractured that rib on my board last month. You just set the healing process back another few weeks."

"Sorry," I said, grimacing.

"It's Sutter now," came my favorite deep voice from right outside our circle.

Corbin, along with the rest of us, turned. Manning had drifted over, still swaying the baby, his eyes trained on Corbin's arm around me.

"Right, right," Corbin said. "It'll take me a while to see her as anything other than a Kaplan."

"Answer the question," I told Corbin, only slightly giddier to uncover the truth than I was to see Manning's reaction to it. "Did you and Val have sex?"

"You need to ease up on the doobies," Corbin said as he mimed sucking on a joint.

"Getting high on her wedding day." Val shook her head. "So sad. No restraint."

Manning had stopped rocking the baby to stare at Corbin and Val, only his eyes moving back and forth. "*Sex*?" he asked. "You two?"

Before I could fill him in, Abby's face scrunched as she raised her fat little arms. Like a ticking time bomb getting ready to blow, she twitched. "Manning," I warned, but it was too late. She let out a wail that made everyone jump.

His eyes widened as he jumpstarted into swaying again. "*Sh*—I'm sorry," he said to Kara. "I didn't—I forgot—"

"It's not your fault," she said with a small laugh, reaching for the baby. "We're overdue for a tantrum."

Manning looked so crestfallen as he handed her over, I couldn't help laughing. "I'm sure you can have her back once she's fed," I reassured him.

My mom touched Kara's back. "It's Abby, right?" she asked, beaming at the baby. "Is she hungry? Tired? Maybe she needs a diaper change."

"All of the above," Kara said. "It's always something."

"Let me help." Mom guided her away as she said, "Tiffany was the fussiest little thing . . ."

I turned back as Val tiptoed away. "Nice try," I called after her. "If you don't cop to whatever the story is, I'm going to make up my own version."

Her shoulders slumped. She slowly rotated back around, as if operated by remote control. "Corbin and I did not have sex," Val said loudly and coughed into her fist, "*today*."

I blew out a laugh. "Liar. Why'd you keep this from me?"

Manning walked around the circle to stand behind me. "Isn't it obvious?" he asked, placing his hands on my shoulders.

"Wait," Corbin said to Val. "Are we doing this now?"

"I . . ." Val put her palm to her forehead. "I guess?"

"Thank *God*," Corbin said, crossing the circle.

Val jumped back, pointing at him. "Don't you dare pick me up. You know I hate it."

"If by hate, you mean secretly love, then yes I know." He wrapped his arms around her waist and spun her.

"My boobs are going to pop out of this dress," she said as she wiggled and squealed. "Put me down."

"No. I've had to keep this to myself for too long." Corbin set her on her feet and puffed out his chest. "Valerie Kristen Jameson is my best friend *and* my girlfriend," he declared loudly enough for people to look over. "If you don't like it, deal with it."

With a dramatic dip, he kissed her. She pretended to push him off but laughed through all of it.

I stood there blinking, Manning's hands warming my bare shoulders. I had no idea what to make of it. My two best friends were kissing, and it looked strange and awkward and wrong. I didn't like it.

Did I?

When Corbin righted her, Val cried, "You know I hate PDA," and started to run away.

He nabbed her by the waist and brought her back in front of him, hugging her middle. "Get over it. After months and months of torture, I'm displaying my affection publicly tonight."

"How did this happen?" I blurted. "Why? Why didn't you guys tell me?"

"We didn't tell anyone," Val said. "We weren't sure what would happen, if it would go well . . . or if we'd make it."

"That's not true," Corbin said. "*This one* wasn't sure. *This one* didn't want to jinx it. *This one* didn't want to steal your spotlight."

"Can you blame me?" she asked, glancing at the ground.

"No, but I want the record to show that even though I'm a blind idiot who took too long to realize what was right in front of me, I was on board with this relationship from the first kiss. I went along with your secrets because you're good at the sex."

"Oh my God," I said, covering my eyes as a naked and horizontal Corbin and Val flashed across my imagination. "Mental images happening. I can't."

"This is why I didn't want to tell you," Val said quietly. "It's weird."

"Lake," Manning murmured in my ear. "Why don't you and Val go talk in the house?"

I slatted my fingers and peeked at the couple. Corbin grinned ear to ear, but Val looked like she was going to be sick.

"I don't want to spoil your day," she said.

"Nothing could spoil today for us," Manning said, massaging my neck. "*Especially* not this news."

Well, at least one person in the group didn't think this was strange. Manning must've been over the moon to finally verify that Corbin had an actual love interest who wasn't me. "Fine, but you—" I pointed at Corbin. "Stay out here. No spying."

Corbin showed us his palms. "All I ever wanted was to eat cake in peace."

Val followed me up the back steps and into the kitchen. She sat at the table as I switched on the overhead light, hiked up my dress, and took the seat across from her. "Let's have it."

"Are you mad?" she asked.

"Mad?" A host of emotions ran through me. I was confused. Weirded out. And somewhere between repulsed and curious. It hadn't really entered my mind to be upset, though. I planted my elbow on the table and my chin in my palm. "No. Why would I be?"

"Corbin was in love with you for so long, and you guys had a thing I never understood." She picked at nothing on the table. "I feel like I should've asked your permission or something, but it happened kind of fast."

"You don't need my permission. Who am I?" I deflated in my chair with a sigh, running my hands down the lace of my dress. "I don't really know how to feel. Just start from the beginning."

"It's a short story, but it goes back a long time. I've always . . ." She laced her hands on the table, then opened one, as if trying to find the words. "I've had a crush on him since high school," she rushed out. "I actually noticed him my first day, but as soon as you introduced us, I could see he liked you, so I sort of ignored how I felt."

"Jesus, Val. I didn't have feelings for him." I

remembered back to that first year in high school when Corbin and I had become friends. I couldn't even really pinpoint why we'd gotten so close, except for his romantic interest in me. "You could've gone out with him."

"Not knowing how he felt about you."

Back then, I'd thought Corbin's crush wasn't a big deal. It'd been easier to ignore it than squash it, but that'd ended up costing all of us in the end, it seemed. "How long have you been together?"

"A few months. Six or eight." She cleared her throat, glancing at the fridge. "Maybe ten. When I say it happened fast, I mean suddenly we were in it and the more time that passed, the harder it got to tell you."

My stomach dropped—not because they'd kept it a secret, but because Val and Corbin were only finding each other now—after over *a decade and a half* of knowing each other. Could they have been together all this time? Was it my fault they hadn't been? "Why not years ago, when I moved in with Manning?" I asked. "Why not in college?"

"So many reasons." She lifted her bare shoulder. "Mostly, after everything you'd been through with Tiffany, I didn't want you to feel like I was betraying you by going after Corbin. So I kept it to myself."

"I wouldn't have thought that." It'd been so long since I'd had any inkling of interest in Corbin, but I had to admit at one time, I'd wanted to love him. I'd wanted to forget Manning and take the easy way out with Corbin. Would I have been upset if he and Val had fallen in love while my heart was broken? I couldn't know for sure, and Val knew me as well as anyone, so maybe she was right. "I'm sorry," I said.

"Don't be. It didn't matter anyway." She bent to remove one of her heels, massaging her foot. "It was so obvious he still had feelings for you."

"But if you'd spoken up, he would've realized sooner."

"I don't think so. Back then I'd wished he'd see me, you know, really *see* me. But looking back, it wasn't our time. He needed to get you out of his system." She smirked as she replaced her shoe. "You, then lots of other girls."

Manning entered the kitchen and set two coffee mugs and a pitcher of creamer in front of us. "I wasn't sure how you take it," he told Val, handing me some sugar packets from his pocket and leaving the rest on the table.

"*Thank you*," she said, ripping one open. "This wedding crap is exhausting. You read my mind."

"He's good at that." My face warmed as I remembered his earlier comment about drinking coffee to prepare for our night ahead.

He winked. Yep—*definitely* a mind reader. "Drink up, *Wife*," he ordered.

"I really love the wedding arch," Val said, balling up an empty packet. "Did you make it?"

"With help from Charles." Manning turned to leave. "Let me know if you girls need a refill."

"How about the food?" she asked. "Was it your idea?"

He paused, looking back. "What?"

"Manning planned almost everything," I said. "Barbeque was his idea. I picked the color scheme, and he designed the ceremony and reception. He made all the arrangements for our honeymoon to the South of France, too."

"Wow. You're a machine, Manning."

"A machine in love," he agreed.

"Ah . . ." Val shifted in her seat, adjusting the top of her dress. "I'm sorry I ever, you know, doubted you."

"I'm not," he said. "You were looking out for her when nobody else was."

"Except Corbin." Val straightened in her seat. "He was always good to her. I feel like you should acknowledge that."

Manning's eyes dropped to mine. Corbin had no longer become a touchy subject between us, but that didn't mean Manning had completely conquered those feelings of jealousy. He wasn't about to concede in that department.

"He knows," I answered for him.

"You and I have spent enough time together now," she told Manning, "but I think a small part of me always worried you'd hurt her again."

"I won't," he said simply.

"Then I guess I can relax."

He turned to face her. "Are we good?"

Val knew all of Manning's and my darkest secrets. She'd been there for most of our relationship, an ear to listen and a shoulder to cry on every time he'd devastated me. But they'd each wanted the same thing for me from the start—happiness. There was no denying I'd found it, and no more reason to fight.

"Just don't give Corbin a hard time."

Manning showed her his palms. "He keeps his hands to himself and there's no problem."

She grinned. "I'll make sure his hands are on me at all times."

He nodded at me. "Need anything?"

"I'm fine. I won't be long."

Once he'd pushed out of the screen door and disappeared down the steps, I said, "You have no idea how happy you've made him with this news."

"He doesn't still get jealous over Corbin, does he?"

"No, not *truly*." I grinned. "But he gets his hackles up when they're in the same vicinity."

"*Dogs*," she said, shaking her head. "All of them. They're literally reduced to their animal instincts."

Val had no idea how true that was for Manning—and how much I *relished* his primal behavior. Or that I planned to encourage it tonight. I shivered, trying to mentally cool down so I could focus on the conversation at hand. "What were we talking about?"

"Nothing. We should probably leave things for now." She stood. "We can get into more detail another time."

At the thought of her ending the story of her and Corbin already, before we'd gotten to any of the juicy details, I was suddenly ravenous for more. *Lots* more. I must've been pretty okay with it after all. "Where are you going?" I cried.

"Nowhere," she said, grabbing a dishtowel from the oven handle. She held it out to me. "You're making me nervous as fuck with that coffee."

I glanced down. I'd completely forgotten I was wearing cream, but fortunately, I'd avoided disaster so far. I took the towel and tucked it into the neckline of my dress, smoothing it down to my lap. "Better?"

"Much."

"Then sit," I demanded.

"We don't have to talk about this today. You should be out there with your guests."

"If you don't tell me everything *right now*, I'll be forced to torture you."

She leaned her hands on the back of her chair, leveling me with a look. "You're a vet, Lake. You wouldn't harm a fly."

"I'm not talking about physical pain." I smiled sweetly. "I'll just describe all the ways Manning and I plan to consummate our marriage."

"Oh my God—*gross*," she said, covering her ears. "Fine! I'll talk."

I laughed, sipping my coffee. "So did Corbin have any idea how you felt?"

"None." She plopped back into the dining chair.

"In New York, I thought Julian was 'the one' and that I'd moved on from Corbin, but the thing was, he was always there when Julian was a dick. It made my feelings for him really confusing."

"And let me guess—Corbin never even *suspected*."

"He lives in his own world," she said, and we each bobbed our heads in agreement. "He was too concerned with what you were doing—and all his side-ass. But when everything went down with the Twin Towers . . ."

I sucked in a breath. Val had been a different person after the terrorist attacks. The news had turned her into a complete mess. "Was that the real reason you left New York?"

"It was awful, Lake. You know; you were there. Forget the fact that it felt like a personal attack on a city we loved, when I realized Corbin could've been there, could've died on some random Tuesday, it terrified me." The tip of her nose reddened. She stood and went to a drawer, most likely to hide that she was getting emotional. "My *feelings for him* terrified me," she said with her back to me. "I had to face the fact we'd never be together, and I needed to move on. So I left."

I twisted in my seat, following her with my eyes. "And then he moved to Los Angeles, too."

"Yes, but by the time Corbin bought his place in Malibu, I'd given up hope on us, not that I ever really had any." She picked out a spoon and turned to lean against the counter. "He had girlfriends. I was busy with work. I stopped pining for him."

Out back, someone raised the volume on what sounded like Justin Timberlake. The bass rattled me while I waited. "*Until . . .?*" I prompted.

"I went over to his house to surf one weekend. Surfing together wasn't unusual, except that we usually met at my place or the beach. And you know I hung out at his house a lot, but for some reason we'd never surfed there." I passed over her coffee mug when she reached for it. "Anyway, we were on his front deck in the early morning, checking the waves and putting on sunscreen. He sort of stopped and asked why I was still single."

"*Ha.* As if he hadn't been by your side through all of it. What'd you say?"

"I made some joke, like, 'I don't know—you tell me. You know me as well as I know myself.'"

"Aww." It was so *true*, though. I was annoyed I hadn't figured them out years ago.

She straightened her back, imitating Corbin's sometimes unfair amount of confidence. "He was like, 'Yeah I do, so what about you and me?' He wanted to know if I'd ever thought about him 'that way.'"

"Ugh." I rolled my eyes. "Guys have it so easy."

"That's exactly what I was thinking," she exclaimed. "As if I hadn't wondered about *us* a thousand times over the years." She stirred her coffee and tapped the spoon against the rim. "Later, he told me seeing me in his house, how comfortable I was there with him, swapping my surfboard for one of his without asking permission—it'd fallen into some vision of the life he'd been trying to find with other girls." Her eyes softened as she looked past me. "Like I belonged there."

I covered my heart. "Someone to go out on the water with."

"I guess? Oh, and get this." She lowered her voice, smiling with a hint of mischief. "I was half-dressed in my wetsuit so I had my bikini top on. I adjusted the string to see if he'd look, and he did. *Finally*, something in his eyes changed, like he was seeing me for the first time."

Val shuddered as I got goose bumps. "I mean, you're super sexy," I said, "so of course he'd noticed that, like, eons ago."

"He says so, but until that day, it'd always been in a brotherly way. Weird-o." She laughed. "I mean, he'd never ogled my tits that way before, so there's that."

"Fifty bucks says he did, you just never noticed." I warmed my hand on my mug. "So what'd you say to all that?"

"I was honest with him." She set the stirring spoon in the sink and took a quick sip. "My heart started beating so hard, I could barely hear what I was saying, but I didn't want to lie. I admitted I'd had a crush on him up until recently."

"How did he react?"

"He wanted to know why I'd never told him. Well, duh—he'd never asked."

"He should've realized," I said. "But then again, I didn't. You're good at hiding it. *Too* good."

"It's all that time I've spent on set," she said, pointing at me. "I'm becoming one of you actor pod people."

"Hey, I got out of that black hole somehow. I'm not an actress anymore." I gestured to hurry her along. "But quit trying to change the subject. What happened next?"

"I tried to play off my crush like it was no big deal." Her posture wilted. "You guys are so fucking important to me. My feelings weren't worth risking your friendship or his." She scratched her calf with her shoe. "So I picked up the surfboard thinking we could forget the whole thing, but he took it from me and set it aside. He could tell I was lying and that it wasn't nothing."

I was nearly falling out of my seat. "And then?"

"He asked if he could kiss me. At first I said no. I didn't want to go back down that path, so I went with the easiest, most hurtful excuse I could think of."

I grimaced, because I had a feeling that "excuse" had to do with me. "What'd you say?"

"That it would never work between us because he'd loved you and probably still did." She straightened back up. "I wasn't going to be anyone's consolation prize."

"He didn't have any feelings for me at that point," I said. "If you'd asked me, I would've told you."

"He said the same. He still says it. It was a problem for us in the beginning," she admitted. "Sometimes it still is. It's hard for me to forget years and years of watching him pine for you."

"I understand that better than anyone," I said, setting aside my coffee to stand. I leaned a knee on the seat of my chair, addressing her so she knew I meant what I was saying. "Corbin and I had plenty of time and chances to try to make it work. We never did, and that means something."

"I know," she said. "I'm getting over it, mostly because he tells me every day how much he loves and appreciates me."

"He says he loves you?" I asked, clasping my hands. "Oh my God."

Her face was uncharacteristically red as she said, "I can't take you seriously with that bib on."

I swiped the towel from my dress and tossed it on the table. "Did you reciprocate? Tell me you've said it back to him."

"I could've right there on the deck. You know how charming he is." She sounded annoyed, but then she smiled. "He got his kiss, and I was in love with him all over again. But I couldn't tell him. It took me a lot longer to get over the fear that he'd leave once I said I loved him . . . but I eventually did, and he's still here."

For not knowing how I felt about this a few minutes ago, I could barely contain my excitement now. "I'm ecstatic." Filled with awe, I sat back against the table's edge. "I'm embarrassed I never saw it, and that I wasn't there for you—but I am now."

"I've been worried about what our friends would say. Mostly you, obviously."

"You want to know what I think?" I gestured to the backyard. "I'll go get the officiant right now. We can make this a double wedding like you wouldn't believe."

She laughed loudly. "Oh, no. I'm not the marrying kind."

I rolled my eyes. She'd said that before, but I'd assumed she just hadn't met the right guy. "You're telling me Corbin's okay with no wedding?"

"Yep." She yawned, clearly in no rush to get down the aisle. Or was it a show? With Val I could never be sure. "We're doing our thing for now."

"But think of how much fun we'd have sharing an anniversary." I picked up my mug, smiling over the rim as I took a sip. "I'd invite you on my honeymoon too, but I'm pretty sure Manning would kill one of us."

She came over, put my coffee down, and hugged me. "Thanks for being supportive. I swear, I never wanted you to find out today."

"Oh, I need in on this," I heard Corbin say a moment before wrapping his long arms around the pair of us. "Are we all good? Val is seventy-five percent moved in to my place, but she wouldn't take the final plunge without you knowing."

I pulled back to look at them. "Are you kidding?

Manning and I will *help* you move in. His truck is a monster. I'll bet we can fit the rest of Val's apartment in one trip."

"I can leave the rest behind," she said, blinking up at him. "Corbin's house already feels like . . ."

He rubbed her back. "Like what, babe?"

"Home, I guess."

I looked around my kitchen. I knew that exact feeling. I had also walked into this home and known it was mine. Since then, it had never, not once, felt like anything other than where I belonged.

Tonight hadn't only been a happily-ever-after for Manning and me. Val, Corbin, and even Tiffany, had each found one, too. From watching the sky move with Manning to telling him forever was too short an amount of time to spend with him, the day had been perfect. And it should've been enough. *All of this* should've been enough.

But deep down, I worried it wasn't.

12

The reception ended just before midnight. My dad had fallen asleep in our living room recliner, so my family was the last to leave. After sleeping apart from Manning the night before, and a full day of being surrounded by company, I was ready for alone time with my husband. It was the only thing keeping me from insisting my family stay in the guestroom rather than the hotel Manning had arranged. That, and I was pretty sure Manning would annul the wedding if I interfered with his impending plans for me in any way.

After I'd spent a few minutes out front recapping the night with my mom and sister, I said goodnight and went to find Manning. He sat facing the wrong way at an empty picnic table out back with a cigar in hand and an exhausted Blue sleeping at his feet.

Except for the fact that we were alone, and even the caterers had left, the party could've still been going. White lightbulbs crisscrossed over the dance floor we'd rented, plastic plates with cake residue dotted the tables, and a mixed CD played on the speakers, though the volume had been lowered to soft background music.

"I thought you'd be picking up," I said as I blew out the remaining lit votive candles we'd arranged down the center of each table.

He rested an ankle over one knee. "I put the cake and leftovers away. The rest can wait until tomorrow."

I continued stacking dessert plates where he'd left off. "I don't think you've ever gone to bed while the house is messy." I winked at him. "No matter how hard I've tried to *tempt* you away."

"Tempt me." He kept his eyes on me. "Maybe tonight's your lucky night."

I dumped the dirty plates in a Hefty trash bag and started nesting name cards. "I don't think it could get any luckier."

After a pull from his cigar, he nodded at me. "Leave that stuff, Lake."

I paused. "I should at least take the presents in."

"Nah. C'mere."

"We won't have a lot of time to clean tomorrow. Our flight leaves in the evening, and it'll take us at least—"

"I'll pay the dog sitter extra to take care of it. Just come over here."

Slowly, I zigzagged through the tables toward him. His impatience visibly grew the closer I got. Blue groaned and twitched. "Did you walk her tonight?" I asked.

"Yep."

"Food?"

"Between the first dance and the cake."

I mock-gasped. "What a good husband."

I stepped over Blue as Manning opened his knees for me to stand between them. He ran a hand up the back of my thigh. "When can you wear this dress again?"

"Never," I said. "This was it."

He squeezed my backside. "Too bad."

"You'll have plenty of time to get tired of it once I hang our wedding photos."

"Not possible." He flexed his hand around the outside of my hip, pressing his thumb close to my pubic bone. "I'm not ready for you to take it off for good," he said, his voice turning gravelly, "but it's also all I can think about."

"Me too." I wrapped my hand around his forearm as butterflies erupted in my tummy. "Maybe we *should* leave this mess for tomorrow."

"No maybe about it." He put out his cigar and stood, towering over me, challenging me with his height, his hungry eyes. "Definitely."

He slipped an arm around my waist and took my hand to sway to "Wonderful Tonight." Blue looked up at us. "We're going to dance a few moments," Manning said, "then I'm carrying you inside."

"You don't need to," I said. "I'll go willingly."

"That's what the groom does at the end of the night."

"I already entered the house as a married woman. A few times, actually. One of the perils of having the ceremony in your backyard."

He grunted. "You haven't been in the bedroom, have you? I'll take you straight to our bed."

"No." I half-smiled, blushing as I teased him. "What does the groom do in the bedroom?"

"The rest's not suitable for Blue's innocent ears." Manning bent, scooped me up into his arms, and walked us up the steps to the house. "Any last requests before we lock ourselves in for the night?"

Arms loosely wrapped around his neck, I closed one eye as I thought it over. "We should probably get water," I said.

"Hydration. Good call. Did you get enough to eat tonight?"

"Between pork, potatoes, and wedding cake, I'd say so."

"We'll bring snacks just in case." He paused at the back door. "Ready to cross the threshold?"

"Do I have a choice?"

"No," he said. "Not according to the Romans."

Blue zoomed ahead of us, clattering through her dog door. "What do the Romans have to do with it?" I asked.

"There are two reasons the groom carries the bride." He readjusted me in his arms. "One is that evil spirits might try to get you through the floor. In my arms, you're protected."

"Aw." I patted his chest. "How sweet. What's the other reason?"

"Back in the day, brides were supposed to act distraught about being married off. Basically," he lowered his forehead to mine, "I'm dragging my unwilling bride into my home."

My stomach clenched with the dip in his voice, his breath near my mouth. "I don't think anyone can argue I wasn't willing," I said.

"Knowing all that, would you rather walk in yourself?"

I got the sense Manning wanted to see this through. On a regular day, there was no place I'd rather be than in his arms—it was only more true of our wedding night. Slowly, I shook my head. Holding each other's gaze, Manning stooped to jiggle the door open. As he walked us through, my skin tingled, my nipples hardening with anticipation for our night ahead.

"Feel any different?" he asked on the way to the kitchen.

"A little."

"Me too."

He set me down on the counter. "Stay there," he said. "Evil spirits might still be lingering." He moved around the kitchen, grabbing water bottles from the fridge, a box of Wheat Thins, and a bag of chocolate chips. "This should do it," he said. "Now we go to the bedroom—but this time, I want your legs around me."

"That's going to be tough in this dress," I said.

"I can help with that." He put the food and water down and squatted at my feet. He took his time removing my boots, dropping them on the ground. As he ran a hand up the outside of my calf, he pushed my dress up with it. "My only regret today is that I didn't get to shave your legs this morning. Spending the night apart was a terrible idea."

As he touched me, I leaned back onto my hands and closed my eyes, only partially aware of what he was saying. "I love you," I said.

"I know you do, my good girl." He moved my dress up higher and kissed the inside of one knee, sliding his palms and the fabric up my thighs. "You're the sweetest of everything," he said. "Better than cake or pie or even cotton candy."

"I doubt that," I said, sighing.

"Then you should taste yourself."

I *had* tasted myself, at Manning's demand, several times. I shivered at the memory of his fingers in my mouth as his hands inched higher, inviting the night air against my skin. "You're going to torture me tonight, aren't you?" I asked.

"I'm going to do everything one man can between sundown and sunrise," he said. "And I'm going to enjoy every moment of it."

"Are we starting here?"

"No. We start in our bedroom." He stood, bunching my dress up around my hips to free my legs. I wrapped them around his waist, sliding up until I felt him hard and long through his pants.

"Get the water."

I picked up a bottle in each hand, wrapped my arms around his neck, and held on. Manning gathered the rest of the food and walked us down the hall to our room. I shifted against his crotch, warming myself up. "You know," I said, pulling myself more tightly against him, "you should be *extra* turned on right now."

"I doubt that's possible."

I kissed his cheek, murmuring, "You're protecting, providing, and mating me all at once. Keeping the evil spirits away. Bringing snacks you foraged from the kitchen, and . . ."

"And?"

"The mating part."

"The best part." He reached our door, which we'd closed off and locked in case any guests had come into the house. "Fuck."

"What?"

"My hands are full, and the key's in my shed."

"Why?"

He dropped the food on the ground. "I didn't want to carry it in my pocket all night."

With my back to the door, I only heard the knob wiggle. "What're you doing?"

"Breaking it."

"Manning." I sighed with exasperation. "You can't go around breaking locks all the time."

"This one's extra strong, too," he said proudly. "Installed by the best—yours truly."

"So let's go find the key."

His bicep flexed against my ribs with the effort. "I can get it."

"You'll splinter the whole thing."

"Then I'll fix it." With a snap, I looked over my shoulder as the door swung open. "There we go."

"The food—"

"I'll go back for it."

"But Blue might get into it."

"That mutt," he griped, nudging the crackers and chocolate into the room with his boot before kicking the door closed. We had to shut it to get alone time, or Blue would interrupt us—we knew from experience.

Manning pushed my back up against the nearest wall. "I want to fuck you in your wedding dress, Lake." His mouth was suddenly hot on my neck, his hands squeezing my ass. "Will you let me fuck you in your wedding dress?"

I let my head fall back, giving him better access to my throat. "I have special lingerie for you."

"And I want to see that, too. I want to taste you everywhere tonight. I want to be wearing your scent like cologne by dawn. But the first time as a married couple, I want your dress on."

I dropped the water bottles. They thudded heavily on the wood floor, rolling under the bed. I answered him by undoing his belt buckle. "Only if you leave your suit on, too."

He held me up by my waist so I could get his zipper down. My mouth watered at the sight of his beautiful cock against the fine fabric of his suit, at his urgency to spoil my cream bridal dress bunched between us. I lined him up against me, sliding his head through my wetness. "You told me once you wanted to blemish me. Ruin me. Now's your chance."

"Careful, or I'm going to rip right through your dress."

"The way you did my innocence?" I asked in his ear.

He pushed me harder up against the wall but didn't enter me. "All I did was claim you. But you were already mine, weren't you, Birdy?"

He started to press inside me, stealing my breath as he made me wait. "Yes," I said, looking up at the ceiling.

"Now it's official. Now, you're mine to lick and suck and fuck—anywhere, any time."

I pushed down onto him, but he slowed me by holding my hips. "Please, Manning."

"Lake."

I took my eyes from the ceiling to look at him. "Please."

"Tell me you're with me," he said. "That you understand what this is, right here—what it means to me."

I breathed through my mouth, my mind racing to keep up. Manning going crazy enough for the both of us, deciding when and how to fuck me, talking me into a frenzy—none of that was new. The difference tonight was that I'd stood in front of everyone we knew and made him mine. "You and I are official," I said to him. "You're my *husband*."

"You're *my* wife. Now tell me what you want."

"I want to be claimed and consumed and made love to by my husband. First against the wall because he can't wait. Then on the bed he built us. *Our* bed."

He thrust halfway in. I arched my back, keeping my eyes on his because he would've demanded it anyway.

"I want us to be married in every sense of the word," I continued.

"Fuck, Lake," he nearly begged, gripping my hips. He was so big that it always took time—and patience neither of us had. "I can't believe, after all these years, I haven't fucked you right open."

I bit my lip, groaning as I urged him deeper, my heels digging into his ass. "You fuck me open *every* time."

Manning plunged the rest of the way in. I held onto his shoulders as he took me, his hot, urgent mouth on mine. His powerful thrusts and skilled fingers brought me to the edge as his lips wandered down my neck. But it was catching sight of us in the floor-length mirror, the groom in his suit, fucking his willing bride in her dress, that brought me to climax.

Manning saw me through my orgasm, then carried me to our bed. He lay me on my back, standing between my legs with determination in his eyes. Still inside me, he slowly rocked his hips back and forth. He hadn't come, and he didn't want to—not yet. We had a long night ahead of us.

That didn't mean I wouldn't try to get him to. I took his tie with both hands, sliding it through one fist and then the other. "How do you want to come, Bear?" I panted. "In my mouth? My ass?"

His eyes darkened. "I've never come in your ass, and you look far too sweet—and I'm far too eager—to start tonight."

"When did any of that stop you before?"

"You want to play?" he asked. "Flip over."

My bravado came from tying the knot, plain and simple. I felt empowered being Manning's wife. But the truth was, we hadn't yet ventured into that territory, even though I knew from some of Manning's heat-of-the-moment dirty talk that he was into it. I'd always figured that day would come, and though Manning had claimed me for real today and was about as turned on as I'd ever seen him, I wasn't sure our wedding night was the right time for this.

"What's wrong, Goldilocks?" he asked, sliding his hands up my thighs and under my dress as he peeled down my thong. "Suddenly scared you wandered into the wrong bear's house?"

I shivered, my nipples firming against the lace of my corset. "I don't know if I'm ready for . . ."

"For?"

"Anal."

He grinned devilishly, tossing aside my panties. "You're not. But get on all fours anyway."

I didn't need to ask myself if I trusted him. If he said we wouldn't do it tonight, I believed him—but what *did* he have planned, then? As Manning removed his boots, I got on my hands and knees, turning away from him. "Why am I in this position?"

"Why do you think?" I heard him whip his belt from its loops, then the rustle of his clothing. "Hike that dress up, Lake."

The belt didn't scare me. He'd sometimes spank me in the heat of the moment, but with his father's history of violence, he'd never hit me—that much I knew. I pulled my dress up over my backside. Manning had seen me in every position, from every angle, and maybe that was why the wedding dress excited us both—it reintroduced a layer of innocence to our sex life that we'd stripped away years ago.

He ran his palm over my ass cheek, then gently slapped it. "Mmm."

"What was that for?" I asked, already breathless.

"Allowing someone to play Justin Timberlake at our wedding."

I started to laugh as I looked back at him but paused. There was nothing funny about the six-foot-five inches of muscular, buck-naked man about to devour me.

I bit my bottom lip as he thumbed my folds apart. "We need a taller bed," he said.

"Why?"

"So I can eat you standing up." He got to his knees, and since his *Lake Special* was still a little too high for him, he urged my knees apart until I was spread and even with his mouth. "That uncomfortable?" he asked.

"A little."

"Then I better be quick." He licked from my clit to my asshole, humming with satisfaction. Within seconds his tongue was buried inside me. I dropped my cheek to the bedspread, grabbing the fabric in two fists. Pleasure tingled up my spine, my face burning hotter and hotter.

Manning splayed his fingers on my lower back and pressed the wet tip of his thumb to my asshole. "This okay?" he asked.

"Yes," I said, partly curious, but mostly too aroused to let him stop.

He breached the tight opening. His hand was so large, his fingers felt as if they spanned halfway up my back. I wanted his mouth on me again, so I backed onto his hand. "Fuck me, Lake. I could finish myself off just watching you from this angle."

"Make me come," I begged. "However you want."

With the slightest pressure, he pushed his thumb inside me, that forbidden spot accepting him easier than I would've thought. The snug fit, the rawness of our wedding-night excitement driving us forward, and his tongue back on me as his thumb pumped in and out would've normally been enough to make me climax—but right then, I needed more.

"Manning?"

"Yeah, Birdy," he said between my legs, his deep voice vibrating through me.

"There's something else I want."

"Tell me."

I got back up on my arms. "I want to make you feel good, too."

"You already do." He kissed me right on the pussy, tonguing my clit. "So good."

I took a breath. He'd already gone caveman on me, but I was ready to bring him to his knees for what I hoped would be the first time over the course of the night. I bit my lip, looking back at him. Maybe it wasn't fair to tease him, but times like this, he made it so easy. "I want . . ."

"What?" He arched a dark eyebrow at me. "Can't read your mind, Lake."

"I want you to come so deep inside me, there's no chance I won't get pregnant."

That did it. His jaw ticked as he set his once hungry, now voracious eyes on me. Drawing his thumb out, he stood. I got up on my knees, holding his gaze as I unzipped the back of my dress and tugged it over my head.

He took one look at my spotless white lace corset and swallowed. "I was the first to claim your virgin cunt, Lake. Remember?"

I shuddered before lying back in a show of submission. I nodded breathlessly, even though the answer was absurdly obvious. "You claimed more of me that morning than any other man could in a lifetime."

He grabbed me under the knees and yanked me to the edge of the bed. "Don't talk about other men when I'm in this state," he warned. "You gave me your heart first, then your body, didn't you, sweet girl? Nobody else got anything."

I shook my head on the mattress, my body vibrating with an intense need only he could fill. "Make it official, Great Bear," I said, echoing my demand for a kiss at the altar. "Take what now belongs to you."

He gritted his teeth. "You were always mine, and you're really fucking *mine* now."

I wouldn't have had it any other way.

Manning made good on his promises of marathon fucking. When he wasn't telling me he couldn't get enough of his new wife, he was showing me—hour after hour until the sun rose.

And I knew in my gut—there was no chance we hadn't conceived.

BEAR AND BIRDY

SPRING 2010

13

One spring evening, something in the air changed. Without actual evidence, I knew we were in labor. I should've had some idea how long it'd been happening, but I'd been conveniently pretending the pregnancy didn't even exist.

Standing at the kitchen sink, I inhaled back a film of tears. I saw Manning before he saw me. He stood at the mouth of the stable, dusk settling around him while he raised his cell as if checking for reception. I could still turn out the kitchen lights and pretend I hadn't come home. That I'd stayed late for an emergency operation, or had stopped by a friend's, or been held up by car trouble. Not that Manning would fall for any of that. Lying to him was nearly impossible, not to mention I owned a perfectly functioning car thanks to his frequent tune-ups.

Manning fisted his hair, then turned to look through the window. Through me. I'd hesitated too long over whether to stay, but Manning didn't waste a second. He started toward the house.

I flipped off the faucet. I hadn't remembered washing my hands, but of course I'd known, somewhere inside, that I wouldn't leave Blue to do this on her own. I didn't want to, not really.

I dried my hands on a dishtowel as Manning came through the screen door. "I've been calling you," he said.

"I turned off my phone this afternoon."

"I hate when you do that."

"I had a lot of work to catch up on," I said. "The faster I get it done, the faster I can come home. Interruptions slow me down."

He crossed his arms. "Some interruptions are worth it."

He wasn't happy with me, and I didn't blame him. These past couple months, though, knowing I was in the wrong hadn't motivated me to change my attitude. Life continued to test us. After some bad news from my doctor, I couldn't muster any excitement about someone else's pregnancy—not even my dog's.

"I know you're still angry at me," Manning continued, "but she's in labor. She needs you."

My throat thickened the way it had moments ago when I'd come into an empty house and *felt* the shift.

I'd been expecting it anyway, considering Blue had lost her appetite days ago.

She needs you.

Blue had needed me for a while, and I'd failed her during her entire pregnancy. I had a choice—go outside and face the truth, or turn and walk away. The latter was much easier, but it was what I'd been doing the past few weeks, and my mood hadn't improved.

"I'll get my things," I said.

"I tried to get her to come in the guest bathroom. I set up a box with clean towels and shredded cardboard like you told me, but I couldn't get her to move."

"She's never spent any time in there. That's not where she's comfortable."

"You might've mentioned that weeks ago when you saw me getting it ready." He stuck his cell in his back pocket. "Is she okay out in the stable?"

"She's an animal, Manning. If her instinct is to be there, then she's fine. You can move the box outside." I turned to leave the room. "And grab a flashlight or something. It'll be dark soon."

I got the whelping kit I'd stocked from a shelf in the garage. Even though Manning had been on edge about everything—the pregnancy, the birth, and what we'd do with the litter—I hadn't mentioned that I'd been preparing.

I went out back to the nearly finished stable, where Manning leaned in one of the stalls. He'd brought the whelping bed with him, but Blue had

187

already created a nest of hay in one corner, where she lay panting on her side.

"She looks uncomfortable," Manning said as I moved around him.

"Well, she's in labor."

I took a step toward her. Blue's eyes shifted to me, but otherwise, she didn't move, not even to wag her tail. "You all right, Blue girl?"

Manning came up beside me. "What can I do?"

"Just stay back and out of the way," I replied.

"Hey." He took my elbow, turning me to face him. "I don't know why you're still so angry after this long, but there's no reason to snap at me."

He was right as usual. Manning had every reason to be fed up with me. I wasn't done being upset, though. With my eyes down, I said, "I'm sorry, but I don't want to argue in front of Blue. It'll stress her out."

Manning released my arm, but his frown stayed with me as I kneeled down. "Hey, girl," I said, slowly reaching out to see if she'd let me pet her. Her tail twitched, relief in her eyes.

That was all I needed to feel the weight of a guilt I'd been avoiding. Up until now, it'd been easy to make this all about me, but seeing Blue this way meant I'd have to put my own insecurities aside.

I pulled on rubber gloves, thinking back to five weeks earlier when Manning had called me out back because Blue had thrown up twice on their morning walk. I'd taken one look at her pink nipples and swollen belly and turned to a concerned Manning. "She's pregnant."

He'd grinned. "Really?"

Looking back, the pregnancy itself irritated me, but it was the excitement in Manning's voice that'd quickly gotten under my skin. "Yes, *really*," I'd said. "I've been asking you for months to bring her by the hospital so I could spay her. Who the hell is the sire?"

"How would I know?"

"Jesus, Manning. *You're* the one who's here with her all day." There were no dogs I knew of in the immediate area. When had Blue even had the opportunity to get knocked up? Manning and I fucked every chance we got and had nothing to show for it but a couple UTIs, a collapsed work table, and an excessive lingerie bill thanks to Manning's proclivity for ripping lace underwear. I'd shaken my head. "Just—never mind."

"Are you upset that's she's pregnant?" he'd asked.

"Am I upset? Of *course* I am," I'd snapped. "There are hundreds of abandoned pets in our county alone, forget the thousands and millions around the world. We're contributing to overpopulation. If we wanted more dogs, we should've gone and rescued them."

Manning had pulled back, his eyebrows halfway up his forehead. "Okay, but it didn't happen that way. Your dog is pregnant. You love animals. You're a vet. How are you not happy about this?"

The licensed vet I'd worked under almost a year constantly reminded the staff to tell our clients to spay and neuter. Since our own pets were a daily topic of conversation, I'd have to admit that I hadn't done it yet. "It's irresponsible," I'd said, then left to get ready for work.

Tonight, for the first time, I tried to summon some excitement about the fact that there were puppies on the way. I patted Blue's rump and pulled out my thermometer.

"Everything looks normal," I said, sensing Manning hovering. "Her water should break soon. You could get her something to drink."

"Sure," he said, his boots crunching on straw as he left.

Alone with Blue, I spoke in soft tones, soothing her as I lifted her tail to take her temperature. Really, she didn't need my help. In fact, aside from stepping back and monitoring the births, there wasn't really anything Manning or I could do. Still, I was glad I'd come home. I wanted to be there for her. Blue was my first real pet, Manning's, too, and she meant the world to both of us. Even if Manning didn't understand my anger, *I* knew, deep down, it wasn't because we hadn't spayed Blue like we should've. I was also to blame for assuming she was never around other dogs when she had acres of land to herself. After the initial shock of the pregnancy had worn off, my embarrassment over not spaying her had become a small part of why I was so upset.

Irrational as it was, all Blue's pregnancy had done was remind me I *wasn't* pregnant. And she was just the latest in a string of brutal reminders. Tiffany was due next month. A receptionist at the doctor's office had recently announced she was having twins. My regular checker at the grocery store had left on maternity leave. Not to mention I often administered prenatal check-ups on animals, ordered ultrasounds, and occasionally assisted in deliveries.

Everybody was getting pregnant.

Every single woman and animal *could* get pregnant.

And then there was me.

Weeks before finding out about Blue, I'd secretly gone to see my gynecologist after a few months of abnormally painful menstrual cramps. Manning and I had been trying to get pregnant for over a year. The instinct I'd had that we'd conceived had flipped to a gut feeling that something was wrong. Manning continued to reassure me he wasn't worried, yet he'd been smoking a lot, sometimes disappearing out back in the middle of the night when he thought I was sleeping. I couldn't blame him for being upset, but even if I asked, I doubted he'd admit he was disappointed things were taking so long.

Now I had an answer.

"I'm concerned you're infertile, Mrs. Sutter."

A pelvic exam and ultrasound had revealed ovarian cysts. My doctor suspected a blocked fallopian tube—my body was keeping Manning's sperm from fertilizing my eggs. Given all that, plus the amount of time we'd been trying, endometriosis was my likely diagnosis. Manning and I had thought we'd moved the stars, but fate would get the last laugh. I hadn't even begun to think about how I'd break the news to him. I wanted to have a solution before I told him—some way of softening the blow. Maybe even a second opinion. Until then, it was easier to be angry, to take it out on him and Blue, to pretend there'd been no ultrasound, no results, and no bad news.

Manning returned to the stable with a dish of water and set it next to Blue. I removed the thermometer from her rectum and checked the temperature. "We're good," I said, noticing movement in her stomach. "And her contractions are starting."

"What now?" Manning asked.

I put the thermometer away, turned, and sat cross-legged to look at Manning. "Now, we wait. It could be quick, or it could be a few hours."

He sat against the wall opposite me, resting his forearms on his knees. "It's late."

"Dogs usually give birth at night," I said.

"I meant you were at work late. You have been a lot lately." He scanned my face, probably reading me like a picture book. Most times, I appreciated his attentiveness, but lately, I wished he'd just stop looking at me. Stop trying to figure me out. There was no good way to tell him that even though I'd fought the heavens for a chance to give us everything we wanted, I wouldn't be able to.

I picked at my cuticles. "It won't be forever."

"I know it won't," he said. "I guess I thought once you graduated, I'd see you more. But maybe that was naïve."

I held my hands open. I didn't know what Manning wanted me to say. We'd been over this before. "Every time we have this argument—"

"This isn't an argument, no matter how hard you try to make it one."

I ignored him. "Every time, I remind you that you've always encouraged me to go to school for what I loved. To follow my dreams."

"And I remind *you* that I'm not upset you have to work. What I hate is that I don't get to see you as much." He pulled at the collar of his flannel. "I want to have dinner with you every night. That was our plan. You promised me you'd never let me work past seven, but you haven't held yourself to that same rule."

I wanted to blame him for Blue's pregnancy and for my missing dinner because he'd encouraged me to do something I loved, but that was my anger talking. It wasn't his fault I'd been dealt a bad hand. I'd once believed there wasn't anything that could keep Manning from me—not anymore. Because he'd let things get in our way before. And I'd fought tooth and nail to make Manning understand he *did* deserve a love story that painted the night sky, that he was enough for me, and that he'd be an amazing parent. Now that he not only believed it, but had let himself want it, I was going to take it away? What would that do to him? To me? To us? Did I owe him the opportunity to walk away, or did he have it in him to take on yet another battle?

"I've only worked through dinner a few times since I started there," I said.

"Nine times in six months."

"I'm still the new kid." I sighed. "I promise it won't become a habit, but I have to prove myself."

"I get it, Lake—I do."

Of course he understood. He had plenty right to be upset that I didn't always come home for dinner when I'd made it clear to him years ago that I wouldn't accept him working a minute after I'd called him to the table. I wanted to be pissed at the universe and at my body for its defects—and at Manning for continually reminding me everything would work out the way it was supposed to.

He was always so goddamn understanding.

At times, it made me angry that *he* wasn't angry with *me*. I *wasn't* understanding.

Blue got up on all fours. Manning also sat forward. "Is she okay?"

She paced around the small space, coming over to sniff me and then Manning. I wasn't sure she registered us beyond the fact that we were sitting there. "Her water broke," I said. "She's getting ready to have the first puppy."

Blue went to her dish, lapped up almost all her water, and returned to her nest—then changed course and lolled into the whelping bed Manning had made.

He blew out a long sigh, as if he'd been holding his breath. Silence stretched as we waited. Even though I'd been through this before, and there really wasn't much either of us could do, my heart began to pound. My girl was having puppies. By tomorrow morning, our family would have grown.

"I think I see something," Manning said after a while.

I straightened up, craning my neck for a better view. "You do?"

"Come here." He opened his knees and gestured for me. "Come watch with me."

I crawled across the hay and sat with my back against his chest. He held me from behind, squeezing me as the puppy crowned.

"Oh my God," I said.

He hugged me to him, probably hearing the emotion in my voice. "Don't you do this for a living?" he teased.

"Yes," I said, "but never with my own baby girl. Thank you for making the bed."

He kissed the back of my head, and we watched, rapt, as Blue gave birth to her first puppy.

"I didn't expect to be proud," Manning said.

Leave it to Manning to feel pride over the birth of a puppy. How would he react to bringing our own child into this world? Could words even describe it?

"I hope you realize I'm going to be in the room when you give birth," he said.

My heart dropped into my stomach. He still held no doubts that time would come. Now, not only was I defective, but I was a liar, too. As long as I didn't tell Manning about my visit to the doctor, I was keeping something important from him.

"You're getting ahead of yourself," I said.

"I just want you to be prepared," he said, laughing. "They'd have to arrest me to keep me away from the delivery room."

The more he spoke, the sicker I felt. If there even was a delivery, it might be years and tens of thousands of dollars away. The next step for us, my gyno had said, was in vitro fertilization. The thought of everything coming our way because *my* body was failing to do its job made it hard to breathe. I shifted to duck out from under him, but he held me where I was. "Where are you going?" he asked.

Anywhere but here. Anywhere I wasn't staring disappointment in the face. "Blue needs more water."

"But you might miss the next birth."

"Luckily there'll be more of them before the night is over," I said.

"Sit with me a second." He pressed the side of his face to mine, his familiar five o'clock shadow suddenly coarse and unpleasant. "Are we okay?" he asked quietly.

"You know the answer to that."

"Yeah. We're more than okay," he said, "but you know it pisses me off when you're pissed at me."

I looked through the door at the stall across from us. When Manning had announced his plans to build a stable in our backyard, I'd giggled like a schoolgirl, teasing him about the time we'd gone horseback riding at camp. What were we going to do with it, though? Despite Manning's help to overcome my fear of riding, I wasn't exactly excited to get back on a horse, let alone own one. I doubted we could even *afford* a horse.

"I'm not pissed," I said finally.

"Then that concerns me even more. If you're not mad, what's been going on with you lately?"

I slouched against him. I'd never be anything but happy with Manning. We'd fought against the odds and won. We'd gotten what we'd wanted, probably more than we deserved. Was it fair to ask for more? "Work stress," I said. "Dealing with people's pets is more emotionally taxing than I thought it would be."

"I love that you care so much," he said. "You can unload on me anytime, though. Maybe I can help."

There he went being compassionate again. I shifted, the straw suddenly prickly through the seat of my jeans. "I just have to get used to it. Things'll calm down."

"Is that all it is?" he asked. "I can't think of anything that would be easier to handle on your own when you could talk to me about it."

I looked back at him as best I could. It was the perfect opening to explain why watching Blue give birth was hard for me, the reasons I'd been shutting him out lately, and the uncertain future ahead of us.

He just looked so proud. So hopeful. These puppies and the onset of spring signified new life, birth, prosperity. I'd have to break his heart soon enough, but it didn't need to be tonight. I angled my chin up, and he kissed me once on the lips. "I'm fine," I told him. "And I love you."

He smiled. "Lucky me."

This time, Manning let me stand. I picked up Blue's dish and walked back to the house wondering how many more times in my life I'd come up against a question nobody should ever have to ask.

Was love alone enough?

14

Eight weeks and five puppies later, Manning and I drove to Newport Beach. One puppy had curled into my lap up front while two more chased each other across the backseat of Manning's truck, barking out the window at everything in sight.

"They're probably anxious being separated from the others," I said, pouting when Manning complained about the noise. He was already annoyed we'd had to stop twice to let them out. "We should've brought them all."

"*All?*" he asked. "We've got enough excitement for a two-hour drive with Tweedledee and Tweedledum back there."

"Stop calling them that."

He laughed, sliding one hand down the steering wheel. "I'll bet money your dad picks the female."

I ruffled my fingers through the furry head in my lap. We'd agreed not to name the pups we were adopting out so we wouldn't get attached, but I'd taken to calling her Lady since she was one of two females in the litter. "We could've at least brought Blue. She's been grumpy, and I don't blame her. She's barely had a minute alone in weeks."

"Sorry to break it to you, but that bitch isn't leaving the house until she's spayed."

I gave Manning a reproachful look. Just because my anger with him had fizzled the moment I'd held Blue's first puppy didn't mean I'd forgotten anything. He was lucky I'd been too busy to stay mad at him. Not only had our sleep been compromised while potty-training five puppies at a time, but April had kicked off the most hectic quarter I'd seen since starting at the animal hospital. And, it was hard in general to be sad with a houseful of puppies. "Blue should be healed enough for the operation by now. We're swamped at work, but—"

"I'll bring her, even if I have to sit in the waiting room for hours," he said with an exaggerated grimace. "You have my word."

Lady looked up at me with icy blue eyes like her mom's. "I don't know, Manning. Maybe we should just . . ."

"Don't even think about it."

"We could keep them all," I said with excitement, in hopes it'd rub off on him. "They're a family."

Manning barked a deep laugh that made Dee and Dum go still in the backseat. "You didn't even *want* them in the first place."

I covered Lady's ears. "Shh. Don't let them hear you say that."

"Christ." Manning stretched an arm along the back of my seat, absentmindedly touching my hair. "And what'll everyone think if we show up to a— what'd you call it?"

"A puppy party." I smiled. I'd co-opted Sunday dinner and invited Manning's and my closest friends to my parents' house to adopt a dog. Fortunately, they all seemed into the idea, because I hadn't really given them much choice.

"What happens when we show up to a puppy party with no puppies?" Manning asked.

"I don't think I care." I held up Lady to Manning's profile. "Do you see this face?"

"All I've seen the past month are big ol' puppy-dog eyes, and not just from the dogs." He arched a scolding eyebrow at me. "How you talked me in to keeping two of them, along with Blue, I'll never understand."

"With names like Altair and Vega, how could they not be ours?" I picked white fur off the Pink Floyd concert tee Manning had bought me when we'd seen Roger Waters live a few years earlier. "They're two-thirds of Summer Triangle."

"You do realize they didn't come out of the womb with those names . . ."

I huffed. "It was always in the plan to have lots of animals. You knew that."

"Over a lifetime, yes. Not all at once." He sighed. "I'm dreading explaining three dogs to your dad. He's going to think I'm some kind of pushover."

I didn't want to break it to Manning that when it came to me, especially where puppy-dog eyes were involved, he *was* a pushover. "Oh, fine," I said, picking up Lady for some kisses. "We'll have to come visit every weekend then."

Manning flipped on his turn signal, shaking his head. "First, you get mad Blue's pregnant, then you want to keep the entire litter. Now, you want to pay four visits a month to the family you didn't speak to for over a decade." He grunted but twirled a piece of my hair around his fingers. "Talk about a moody bitch."

"*Hey,*" I said, smacking his chest as he laughed.

———

Manning and I had barely leashed the puppies when Gary opened my parents' front door. The dogs ran circles around us, tangling their leashes as they sniffed out where to go to the bathroom.

"Are we late?" I asked, trying and failing to check my watch as Tweedledee pulled my arm taut. "I was going to walk you guys in since you don't really know my parents that well."

Lydia ducked under Gary's arm. "It's fine," she said with a dismissive wave. "We talked to your parents at the wedding. I wanted to have first pick of the litter."

"You can't go wrong with any of them," I said. "Although, they *do* have personalities."

"Which one's a beach dog?" Gary asked, coming down the walkway. "I need a surfing pal."

"*Surfing*?" Lydia asked him. "As if I need more sand in the house. Which one's *not* a beach dog?"

"Welcome to your future," Manning said, passing Gary a plastic bag and pointing to Dee's pile of poop. "Get scooping."

My mom came to the door, waving us in. "What're you doing out here?" she asked. "Everyone's in the den."

"The puppies are full of energy," I said, hiking up my jeans by the belt loops. "They need to do a few laps around the block."

Manning handed me Lady's leash to help Gary. "It's been a while since you've had kids in the house," he said to my mom as he pulled another plastic bag from the back pocket of his jeans. "Are you sure you're ready for this?"

"We've never had a dog," she answered, and with far less enthusiasm than I'd hoped for. "Except that one that died when Lake was seven."

"Mom, please," I hissed, picking up Lady while tugging the other puppies up the front steps and into the foyer. "They can understand you."

Her eyes went wide. "They can?"

"Yes." I set Lady down and hung my purse on a hook. "Dogs can read moods. They're very sensitive. Death might depress them."

"Bullshit," Dad said, coming out of his study. "Don't tell me you buy that, Cathy."

"Well, Lake *is* a vet."

"Exactly," Dad said. "She should understand that these are animals with one purpose: *survival*. They do not have emotions. They're not teddy bears." He stooped to pick up Lady, the calmest of the three, and held her in front of his face. "I could say this one's going to be nothing but a nuisance in this household, and she wouldn't understand a thing I said."

"She senses your energy, Dad—whether you're scared, happy, distressed."

He *tsked*. "I'm surprised to hear that from a science-minded woman. Next you'll tell me you believe in Tarot cards or magic or psychics. Nonsense."

I glanced out the front door at Manning. He and Gary walked their bagged dog shit down to the garbage cans at the curb. I rarely had to pick up after the pups; Manning always beat me to it. He was my domestic hero and sexier than ever. There had to be a word for that—my ability to find him irresistible, and to love him fiercely, while he handled poop. "Magic," I said under my breath.

Dad snorted, examining Lady's underbelly, her paws and snout. She let him without protest, her eyes glued to his face. "This one's a mutt."

"Of course she is." I crossed my arms. "They all are. We got Blue from the pound and we think she's a mix of Border Collie and Australian Shepherd."

"Which one's ours?"

"Why not her?" I asked. Manning had already determined they'd be a good fit, and it seemed he was right. "That's the one you chose."

"I just picked up the first one I saw."

"Then she chose you."

He frowned at her. "What's her name?"

"I've been calling her Lady to keep things orderly," I answered, "but you can choose something else if you want."

"Well, well." He cocked his head at her as she wagged her tail, and for a moment, I thought he might actually cuddle her. Instead, he set her down. "Go on," he said, but she sat on her haunches, looking up at him. When he took a step, she got up. "What's she want?"

"Either she's trying to herd you into the kitchen for food, or she likes you."

He turned on his heel. "You're anthropomorphizing again."

"And *you're* doing a good thing, Dad," I said, following him through the house. "You and Mom need some excitement around here."

"Between you and your sister, I've had enough excitement for one lifetime. This is your mother's project, not mine." In the kitchen, Manning washed his hands at the sink. "How's business up there in Big Bear?" Dad asked.

Manning's shoulders rose. Lately, he seemed more and more stressed whenever work came up, but I'd convinced myself it was my imagination. He'd hired a couple extra hands before Thanksgiving and had even admitted it'd been a good decision. Higher productivity freed Manning to accept more orders.

He turned, swiping a paper towel from its roll. "Better than ever."

"You say that every time you're here," Dad pointed out.

"It's true," I said.

He nodded. "That's what I like to hear."

Manning balled up the towel. "I've been thinking of branching out a little. Maybe trying to get a crew together to look into some construction jobs around town."

I drew my eyebrows together. "I didn't know that."

"I've mentioned it," he said, still addressing my dad. "I'm only now getting serious about it."

"But you love making furniture."

"Doesn't mean I can't be a contractor, too." He glanced at me and then away. "Having help has opened up opportunities."

I didn't doubt that, but why hadn't I heard about this until now? Before I could push the issue, my dad said, "I think it's smart. Time to scale. That's how you'll make the real money."

"We do very well," I said to my dad. "Manning's already making more than he did when he worked for you."

"You don't say?" Dad clapped his hands together. "This calls for a celebratory drink. What're you having, Manning? Robby's drinking a 'mimosa' because apparently, Tiffany is engaged to a sorority sister."

Manning straightened his back, his chest out. "I picked up a bottle of Booker's on the way in, sir."

I stifled a laugh thinking of Manning's earlier comment about not wanting to be a pushover. "Tiffany's here?" I asked. "She said she didn't want a dog."

"That's not true," Tiffany called from the den. "I want one, but Robby's allergic."

I left the kitchen. The puppies were already zooming around my dad's favorite recliner, where a nine-month-pregnant Tiffany sat. I'd never seen my sister with such naturally rosy, full cheeks. "Wow," I said, standing in the doorway. "You really do have that pregnant woman's glow."

"I know—I'm a heifer. I look ten months pregnant. I don't know what to do about it."

"What *can* you do, sweetie?" Robby asked from the couch, where he'd huddled against one of the arms. He waved his champagne glass at me. "Afternoon, Lake."

"Hi, Robby. You're allergic to dogs?"

"Some," he said, glancing around the room. "I really shouldn't stay long. I just didn't want Tiffany driving."

"I can drive fine," she said. "Will you get me some water, honey?"

"Sure." Robby stood, smiling at me on his way to the kitchen. "Isn't she glowing?"

I took his spot on the couch to be close to my sister. "How are you feeling?"

"Annoyed," she said. "I might actually be willing to ditch Robby and his allergies for a puppy."

"You don't mean that," I said. "I've never seen you so in love."

"I was until week twenty-five," she said, palming her belly. "Now I hate his guts."

"Oh, please. I'm sure he's been nothing but wonderful."

"Too wonderful. I can't get five minutes alone. Do you think you could sneak one of these dogs into our car?"

Before I could respond, Val walked in, squealing when she nearly tripped over Tweedledum chasing his tail. "Oh my God," she said, bowing her legs to dance around him. In a floppy wool hat and plaid top tied at her belly button, she hooked her thumbs in her belt loops and jigged. "Did I die and go to heaven? Which one is mine?"

"They haven't officially been assigned yet," I said, laughing at her. "Except maybe the female. I think she's attached to my dad. In fact, I haven't seen her in a few minutes."

She glanced at her reflection in the black TV screen, adjusting her hat. "I saw Manning in your dad's study with a dog when I came in."

"Great." I rolled my eyes. "They'll be in there all day. Where's Corbin?"

"Talking to your mom and Gary." Val scooped a puppy off the ground and flopped onto the couch next to me. She paused when she noticed Tiffany. "Holy shit. Is it supposed to be that big?"

Tiffany did her best to cover her stomach—which meant basically resting her hands at the crest of it. "Yes. No. I don't know. Robby says it's normal, and he's a doctor."

"I thought he was an acupuncturist."

"I never said that," Tiffany snapped. "He's a board-certified physician and one of the top pediatricians in Orange—"

"Tiffany, she's messing with you," I said. "Just like she always does."

"Sorry. I can't help it." Val sparred with Dum, who kept biting her fingers. "I can be annoyingly sarcastic sometimes. I use humor as a defense mechanism."

Tiffany and I blinked at her. "What?" I asked.

"I think she's doing the sarcasm thing again," Tiffany said out of the side of her mouth.

"I'm not." Val shrugged. "I've been doing a lot of introspection lately. And talking. Corbin and I talk *a lot.* You'd think we'd have run out of topics after sixteen years of friendship, but nope."

"And he said you use humor as a *defense mechanism?*" I asked. "That doesn't sound like him."

"No, I figured that out on my own when I was *ten*, Lake. It's not rocket science. Corbin doesn't like when I make too many jokes during serious discussions, though." She sat back, staring at Tiffany's stomach. "Some jokes are fine. But anyway. Enough about me. Is it painful?"

"Is what painful?" I asked.

"That." Val pointed at Tiffany. "You look like an overripe tomato."

Tiffany pushed herself up as much as she could in the lounger. "It's mostly uncomfortable. Like, unbearably uncomfortable. There are things happening in my body—and coming out of it—I don't even know how to describe."

Val paled. "Gross."

I smacked her arm. "Pregnancy is a completely natural and *beautiful* time for a woman."

"Does Robby help?" Val asked, rubbing her bicep.

"As much as possible. Since he has to work a lot, he's always sending me to the salon to get my hair blown out, or for pedicures. I mean, they're a complete waste because I can't even *see* my feet. I only go so they'll massage them."

Val blinked a few times. "But it doesn't hurt?"

"Not really," Tiffany said. "It feels funny when she kicks."

Val's back went straight as a rod. "It's a girl?"

"Yep. Thank God," Tiffany added. "I mean, either would've been fine, but now I get to buy her cute outfits."

"Lake, why didn't you tell me?" Val asked.

"I . . ." I studied Val. She had to have some angle for being nice to Tiffany, but I couldn't figure out what it was. "I didn't know you'd care?"

"Have you picked a name?" Val asked.

"Not yet."

"Have you at least narrowed it down?" I asked. "Last time we talked, you had a list of forty or so ideas."

"I tossed them all. Every single one." Tiffany rolled her neck, stretching it side to side. "Nothing sounds right so far."

"How about naming her after Grandma Dolores?" I teased, knowing Tiffany hated the name.

Val made a gagging noise. "Oh, God."

"Hey," I said, scoffing at her. "You know my middle name is Dolly after my grandma."

"No, it's not that," she said, swallowing audibly as she moved Dum off her lap. Her complexion hadn't warmed, and she did look a little pasty.

"Are you okay?" I asked.

"I was thinking about the whole process— getting pregnant, carrying it around for nine months, and then this like, *thing* comes shooting out of your *vagina* like a football." Val shuddered. "How is that normal?"

"At least you aren't a dog. Blue had this thing we call a 'water sac' hanging out of her vulva for an hour before she pushed out five sticky little puppies in a row—"

"I think I'm really going to be sick," Val said, dropping her head between her knees.

"Geez." I leaned down to put the back of my hand against her clammy forehead. "What's the matter?"

"Should I get Robby?" Tiffany asked.

"No. I'm fine." Val shook her head. "I mean, I'm not, but I'm not supposed to say anything—but who cares, right?" She sat up again. "I'm freaking out, Lake. Can you tell? Like really freaking out."

I'd never seen Val so frazzled, and I'd been with her at her worst. "How come?"

"I took a . . . ugh." She removed her hat to fan herself, her spiral curls flapping with the breeze. "I should probably wait for Corbin to announce this."

"I'm here," he said from the doorway between the den and kitchen. He smiled at Val. "Go ahead, babe."

"But it's less than twelve weeks," she said. "Isn't that bad luck?"

I dropped my jaw. It wasn't possible. As far as I knew, Val didn't even want kids. But apparently, that was becoming the quickest path to have them. "You're . . .?"

She nodded. "Pregnant."

I should've squealed with joy, or leapt up to hug my two best friends, or even acknowledged what she'd said. Instead, I stared at her with an open mouth. I didn't see her as Val right then, the girl who'd befriended me when I'd needed someone in my corner. The one who'd always pushed me to be the best version of myself, even when I was at my worst. My best friend in the entire world. I only saw another person who'd gotten something she hadn't even wanted—something *I'd* wanted. And all I could think was . . .

Are you fucking kidding me?

15

Val twisted her hands in her lap, rushing out an explanation, as if she felt guilty. "I don't know if I'm pregnant for sure. I missed my period, so I took a test and it was positive." She shifted on the couch. "But we haven't been to a doctor yet. It could be a false alarm."

"Oh my God, come by Robby's office," Tiffany said. "Our kids will be friends. Even if we're not!"

"It was an *accident*," Val said to me as if she needed to explain. "Corbin and I are still getting to know each other."

"You've known each other forever," I said, my voice sounding distant and foreign even to my own ears.

"Not this way. We've only been dating a year and a half." She and Corbin exchanged a look. "I'm not ready, I know I'll fuck it up—I mean, I just said *fuck* and Tiffany's baby probably heard it through her stomach—she has ears by now, right?" She paused, as if expecting one of us to answer. "I don't even know," she continued, "because I'm completely clueless about this kind of stuff. Oh my God. I'll be a terrible mom."

"I'm not worried," Corbin said, tucking his hair behind his ear with a shrug. "We're going to be killer parents, Val."

The calm confidence in Corbin's voice should've soothed all of us, but Val still looked sick. And me? My palms were getting clammy, too. Was I supposed to feel better that this was an accident? Because somehow, that seemed worse. She didn't even want this baby. But I did, and so did Manning, and we'd been through a lot. We needed this. We had ways of molding the universe to meet our demands, so why couldn't we do it? How was that fair?

Was there anyone who *didn't* get knocked up at the drop of a hat? At this rate, the people in my life were going to overpopulate the entire west coast.

"You going to ralph again?" Corbin asked Val.

She shook her head. "I think it's passing."

"I'll get you a ginger ale," he said, heading for the kitchen.

Val kept looking at me as if gauging my reaction. This wasn't about me. It wasn't. It couldn't be. She hadn't done this to hurt me, but it sure felt that way. I moved my hand, which felt about fifty pounds, and put it on her knee. "Don't worry. You're going to be great. And new moms are supposed to fuck up, so you're basically a natural."

"You better decide if you're getting married now or after," Tiffany said. "You don't want to look like I do on the most important day of your life."

"We're not getting married," she said.

Tiffany wrinkled her nose. "*Ever?*"

"Ever." Dee and Dum ran circles around the couch, stopping every few seconds to whine at us. "It's a dumb tradition. No offense, but it's not for me."

"I want to be a wife as much as I do a mom," Tiffany said, shrugging. "But whatever. I guess Lake is the only one doing it the right way."

Yet I'd been the only one ready and willing—and *actively trying*—to do it out of order. "There's no right or wrong way," I said quietly.

"Corbin was such a playboy for so long," Tiffany said. "I can't picture him as a dad."

"Me neither," Val said.

I could. Corbin had been ready to shed the bachelor life years ago, and from what I'd seen firsthand at Young Cubs and heard about baseball camp, he had a way with kids. Just like Manning. Manning—where was he? He would find out about this, and what would he think? How could he hear Val was pregnant and have any other reaction than to wonder why I wasn't? How much longer until he started to question what was wrong with his wife?

I breathed through my nose to regulate my heartbeat. I couldn't stop staring at Dum as he gnawed and tugged on Val's pant leg. I was a bad friend. I should've been more excited for Val, or probed into the fears I knew she harbored about marriage, or made her admit she *could* see Corbin as a dad, because she'd definitely lied about that. But I couldn't bring myself to do anything but feel sorry for myself.

"I better take the dogs out again," I said, needing fresh air as much as a moment to myself. Somehow, I managed to stand on stiff legs. "My mom'll have a fit if they pee on the new rug."

"Want me to do it?" Val asked, bending down for Dum. "I mean, let's be honest, I think this one is mine."

"No," I exclaimed, snatching him before Val could. He wasn't hers. Not yet. "I'll only be a second. Sit with Tiff in case her water breaks or something."

"Not in your father's favorite chair," my mom called from the kitchen.

Tiffany scoffed. "You're putting me on labor watch? I can't get a second alone as it is."

Val tilted her head at me. "Are you okay?" she asked, her expression dripping with pity.

"Totally. I'm so happy for you." I smiled, leaning over to hug her as the puppy squirmed between us. "I just can't believe it. Congratulations. I'm . . . so happy for you."

I was losing the ability to hold myself together, repeating myself and fighting off tears. I turned to leave so fast, I almost mowed over Corbin. "Whoa-a-a," he said, stumbling back.

"Sorry," I muttered, dodging around him. I whistled for the other puppies. Lady bounded out of my dad's study and met us at the back door. When I let them loose and set Dum down, they went galloping across the backyard as I latched the pool gate. I went around the side of the house to get plastic bags from the recycling bin, then returned to sit on a short wall hiding the pool pump.

Tweedledee and Tweedledum tussled, somersaulting around the grass. Was this my future? Seeing my sister, cousins, friends, acquaintances through their pregnancies? Hiding my gynecologist visits from my husband? Raising Blue's litters? If so, maybe we didn't need to spay her after all. Would these puppies be my only babies? And here I was, giving them away.

"I'm concerned you're infertile, Mrs. Sutter. Based on the information you provided and the cysts I found, it appears to be endometriosis. Let's discuss your next steps."

Just remembering my doctor running through our options, my uterus ached. I pressed my hand against my lower abdomen, trying to ease the throb. I thought back to all the times I'd asked Manning to love me. Choose me. It never occurred to me I might not be able to give him a family.

The backdoor opened and closed behind me. I kept my eyes on the dogs and tried to muster a smile. Otherwise, Manning would start asking questions—but it turned out to be Corbin who'd come looking for me.

He handed me a can of ginger ale. "You looked a little sick yourself."

"Thanks," I said, flicking the tab.

"Are you pregnant, too?" He sat on the wall. "Because that would be pretty dope if you guys had babies at the same time."

"No." I opened the can and took a long fizzy sip that made my nose tingle. In the silence that followed, I realized how curtly I'd answered him. "But I'm so happy for you guys."

"You said that already. A few times." He bumped me with his shoulder. "Is there some reason you wouldn't be happy?"

I peered into the can as if it held all the answers. "Of course not."

"Yeah, because this kid is practically yours. You'll be like its second mom."

"I know." I smiled thinking about how the baby would surely come out tan and blond like his or her mom and dad. It was a warm, sunshine-filled thought until reality came crashing down. Manning's son or daughter probably would've been the opposite. Dark. Pensive. A presence that turned your head.

"You okay?" Corbin asked, rubbing my back.

I tried to answer, but my throat was too tight. I shook my head, forming a fist against my thigh.

"This isn't about us, is it?" he asked. "Haven't you and Manning talked about kids? Is he being a dick about it?"

"No. It's not that. We're ready."

"Are you scared?"

"No more than any normal person would be." I would be a natural mom. I'd always felt that way, which was why not being able to get pregnant seemed so wrong to me. I rubbed my nose. "I'm not scared, actually."

"Then what is it?"

I toed the grass with my Converse. Though Manning and I had acknowledged here and there that pregnancy was taking longer than we'd expected, I hadn't talked to anyone but my doctor about the endometriosis. "I don't know."

He leaned his elbows on his knees. "So you've been trying?"

"Since before the wedding."

Lady rolled around on the grass as Tweedledee flopped down next to her, panting.

Corbin counted on his fingers. "Is that longer than normal to not get pregnant?" he asked. "I don't know anything about this."

"Kaplan women are extremely fertile," I said, imitating my dad's voice.

"Oh, fuck that, Lake," Corbin said. "It doesn't mean anything."

"Except it does. We actually threw out the birth control over a year ago." I twisted my lips, then drank a little more soda. "It's longer than normal."

I didn't want to mention the doctor's visit, to say the diagnosis aloud. It would make it too real, and Manning was the only person who needed such intimate details about my health. "It's not going to be an easy path for us . . . if it happens at all."

"No way," he said. "You're meant to be a mom, Kaplan—sorry—*Sutter*. I feel it in my gut."

"And *my* gut says something's wrong."

"Ignore it." Corbin rubbed his palms together. "It'll happen for you. You're good at going after what you want. Nobody can deny that."

That was true, and hadn't it paid off in the past? This wasn't the time to surrender, but the alternative was armoring myself for another uphill battle. "Sure."

"Have you guys discussed adoption?"

"Me and my doctor?"

"You and Manning."

"Oh. No."

"But you're so passionate about rescues—"

"We're talking about babies, not dogs." The idea of adoption hadn't even entered my thoughts. I wasn't ready to consider alternatives. So, I supposed that meant I wasn't giving up just yet. "I don't think Manning would go for it." *Protect, provide, mate.* "He wants his own children."

"He said that?" Corbin sounded surprised. "That's kind of shitty considering it's not really something you can control. And since when is adopting not the same as having a child?"

"No, no," I said quickly. "He didn't say that, and of course we feel that way. Especially considering his relationship with his aunt and Henry. I know it's not what he wants for us, though."

Corbin took my soda and sipped. "Is he not being supportive? Because I can talk to him. A buddy of mine in New York is going through the adoption process."

With my palms on the wall, I dug my nails into the concrete. "We haven't talked about it yet, the possibility of a problem. Definitely don't bring it up."

"You haven't *talked about it?*"

"No." I pulled back. "It's not something you just come out and tell your new spouse. 'Sorry I'm barren, but you're stuck with me now.'"

"Hey. Come on." He put an arm around me, nestling me into his side. "You're not barren."

Corbin wouldn't be so optimistic if he knew what the doctor had said. I was tempted to unload it all on him, but that wouldn't be fair to Manning. The backs of my eyes heated with unshed tears. "What if I am? How do I tell him?"

"That dude is obsessed with you and everything you do. He'd *never* feel stuck with you—but I guarantee he'd hate that you're going through this alone. Tell him."

"But—"

"*Tell him.* Let him be there for you."

"He'll be so disappointed." A few tears slid down my cheeks, and I wiped them away, frustrated. "We've been talking about this since New York, Corbin. Before we were even official. We want children, and for him, it's like a biological *need*."

"He'll have to get over it." Corbin kissed the top of my head. "What other choice does he have?"

We sat that way watching the dogs for a few more minutes. There was nothing else to say. Corbin couldn't change the situation, and the more I talked to him about it, the more real it became. I had to be honest with Manning. He would want to know, and besides, we needed to start discussing our options. Just because one door might be closed didn't mean it was all over for us.

"You don't really tell Val she makes too many jokes, do you?" I asked.

He chuckled. "Humor as a defense mechanism?"

"Yep."

"I never said that. But I do want us to connect on all levels, and sometimes that means she has to drop the act." He pinged the tab of the can with his thumbnail. "I'm guilty for not *seeing* her earlier than I did, but I also think she didn't want me to. She tried extra hard to keep me from knowing how she felt."

I nodded slowly. "Even *I* didn't know. How do you feel about not getting married?"

"Honestly?" He handed me back the ginger ale and straightened up to pull his hair back into a ponytail. "I like the idea of doing the whole big thing like you guys, but it's not a deal breaker for me. If she doesn't want it, it's cool, as long as she isn't going anywhere."

I squinted at Dum as his front half disappeared into a bush. He wagged his tail and whined, trying to get to something. Probably a lizard. "Are you sure she doesn't want it?"

"No." He shrugged. "She's fucked up over her dad leaving her mom. She's scared. She even talked about having an abortion."

I lost my breath a little. It wasn't all that surprising—she'd always valued her independence. And even though it was painful to think she might decide *not* to have a baby when I didn't have that choice, I had no right to judge her. The day Manning had left New York, Val had gotten me to Planned Parenthood for a morning-after pill when I'd rather have cried myself to sleep. Maybe that'd been my only chance to have Manning's child. Or maybe I'd always been broken. My gut smarted.

"Sorry," Corbin said. "That was probably insensitive considering what you're going through."

I tried to push my own feelings aside because Val was my family. I knew from our conversations that she was in it for the long haul with Corbin. "She's just scared."

"I know."

"Please tell me you talked her out of it."

"Can't talk that girl out of anything," he said. "I had to let her get there on her own, but I knew she would. We're having this baby."

"Wow." I blew out a breath and with it, a tiny bit of my resentment. "I can't believe it."

"See what I'm dealing with? Heavy stuff." He shook his head with a laugh. "The deeper it is, the funnier she seems to get."

"Ah. The defense mechanism." I elbowed his arm, purposely avoiding the ribs this time. "You're right. Maybe a few less jokes would do her good."

"I think so," he agreed, hopping off the wall to stretch above his head. "Anyway, ain't nothing funny about unplanned pregnancy."

I shielded my eyes from the sun to look up at him, and we both broke into laughter. Maybe it was a tiny bit funny.

I finished off my drink and called for the dogs. When Corbin opened the back door, they sprinted inside. Manning wasn't in the kitchen or study, so I returned to the den. While Val and Tiffany compared notes on morning sickness, my dad read the Sunday paper in a recliner next to Tiffany's.

He lowered the paper. "Lake," he said when Lady sat by the chair, "this one won't leave me alone."

I picked her up to put her on his lap. She immediately climbed over the paper, crinkling it as she turned in a circle and settled down. "She likes you," I said.

He hummed. "It would seem so."

Two arms wrapped around my waist from behind, and Manning pulled me against his front. He rubbed my tummy with his thumb, and I could practically hear his thoughts. "Val's pregnant?" he asked in my ear.

"It's not confirmed yet," I said. "But probably."

He swayed us side to side. "There are puppies and babies everywhere."

As if I hadn't noticed. I clenched my teeth to keep a response inside that would only sound bitter or defensive.

"What'd you say her name was?" Dad asked, his hands open and hovering as if he wasn't sure what to do with her.

"She doesn't have one."

He inspected her. "You know, Lake wasn't the name I would've chosen for you. Since I picked Tiffany, I let Cathy decide yours. But I always liked the name Rebecca for some reason."

Lady wagged her tail as she lifted her head to look at him.

"So call her Rebecca," Manning said. "I think she likes it."

My dad finally rested his hand on her back to pet the length of her. "Silly name for a dog."

"I don't think so," I said. "I like it. It's original."

"Rebecca." Dad sighed. "Fine then. She can be Rebecca."

Manning tightened his arms around my middle. "Picking out names is fun, eh? You ever think about that?"

I couldn't breathe, but if I didn't play along, Manning would know something was wrong. Even though the truth bore down on us, I wasn't about to reveal my shortcomings to him here in front of all our friends and family. "Sure," I said.

He lowered his voice. "Got any frontrunners for our baby cub?"

Goosebumps were my natural response to the excitement in his voice. Just talking about babies did all kinds of things to Manning. It turned him into Papa Bear. Protective, primal—and horny.

"No favorites yet," I said, hiding the emotion in my voice. "I don't want to get ahead of myself. Let's wait, okay?"

"Whatever you want, beautiful." He nuzzled my temple, rocking me as we stood puzzled together, a seemingly strong unit to everyone around us—even Manning—but with a very crucial piece missing.

16

Manning and I drove out of my parents' cul-de-sac after dark. We weren't the only ones leaving the beach on a Sunday night, but even without traffic, I suspected the drive home still would've felt longer than the one up. It was definitely quieter.

"What're you thinking about over there, Birdy?" Manning asked.

I spun my wedding ring, picturing its soothing, pearly stone in the dark. "Just how empty it feels."

"The puppies are in great hands," he said. "Val was excited. Lydia would've taken two if she could've. Even your dad fell in love with Rebecca. You should be proud of yourself. And happy."

The way he said *happy* made me think he could sense that I wasn't, but that didn't surprise me. Manning always seemed to know how I was feeling, sometimes before I could even name it. "I'm tired, that's all."

"You've been quiet since before dinner. Did you really want to keep the puppies? I thought you were joking."

"No. There's no way we could handle raising five all at once."

Manning didn't speak for a few miles, long enough for me to assume he'd dropped whatever he was getting at. Deep down, though, I knew he hadn't, so I wasn't surprised when he broke the silence again.

"Then it has to be about Val's news."

I closed my eyes. I didn't want to talk about this. I didn't want to think about it anymore. I didn't want to *feel* like such a failure. Why couldn't he ever just leave it alone? For the first time in my life, I wished he didn't love me *so* much, didn't try to protect me from everyone—even myself. "I'm happy for them."

"I know you are."

"So can we leave it at that?"

"You know we can't," he said.

"I have a headache." I stared out the passenger side window as the landscape changed from breezy, lively Newport Beach to the dark, still mountains. Manning and I had taken this drive many times, but none would ever be as thrilling as the first. The night we'd driven into town, around perfect neighborhoods, and into unforgiving woods, had been one of the best of my life. True, he'd had too many cares and worries for such a young age, ones I'd adopted as my own, but even now, I'd go back, just for tonight. Especially if it meant escaping what lay ahead of us.

Manning didn't push the subject. He let me sulk for the remainder of the drive, but I wasn't off the hook. Not only because Manning wouldn't let me go long in a mood like this, but also because of what Corbin had said. I owed Manning the truth; I just didn't know how or when I was going to tell him.

Around ten, Manning's cell rang. He flipped it open, steering with one hand. "Yeah?" he asked, pausing. "No, it's all right. I'm glad you called." He listened, steering us onto the small road toward the house. "Yeah," he said, his tone wooden. "I understand."

He squinted ahead, ignoring me as I tried to get his attention. "Manning?" I whispered.

"Makes sense," he said into the phone. "It's been a while since I was in the business, so I can't say I don't understand. Keep me in mind, though. Sure." He snapped the phone shut.

"What was that?" I asked.

"Nothing."

"Excuse me?" I asked. "This is a two-way street, you know. If I have to talk about my stupid feelings, so do you."

His nostrils flared as he pulled into our long driveway. "Big Bear's tearing down and rebuilding some public restrooms on the other side of the lake. Joe at the city said he'd put in a good word for me."

I wrinkled my nose. "For furniture?"

"I submitted a bid, but Joe wanted to tell me personally it would be rejected."

"As a contractor? You don't even have a crew."

"I've been getting one together. It's—it *was*—a small job."

"You never mentioned that. I didn't even know you were thinking about any of this until this afternoon."

"Doesn't matter now." He parked and got out, slamming his door shut and starting around the front of the truck.

I hopped down before he reached my side. "Have you submitted for anything else?" I asked as Blue whined from the back gate. After her *accidental pregnancy*, and with so many puppies, Manning had put up a temporary fence.

"Not yet." He went up the porch steps as Blue ran around back to her dog door. "I still need to register as a business, but I wanted to get the ball rolling."

Register as a business? "Are you doing this for real?" I asked. "What about furniture?"

"I can do both." He opened the front door for Blue, and Altair and Vega came tumbling out after her. Manning took their leashes from the foyer. "Who wants to go for a walk?"

Blue went berserk at the word *walk*, and the puppies followed suit, yelping as they ran circles around Manning's boots.

Well, I'd gotten what I'd wished for. Manning was no longer looking at me, trying to read my every last thought, or soothe my worries. He focused on getting the dogs leashed, then stomped down the steps, right past me.

I turned around to watch him go. "What's wrong?" I asked.

"Nothing."

Inside, I prepared three bowls of kibble with raw meat, and waited at the dinner table for Manning. My bad mood had rubbed off on him, and as a result, I felt more guilty than annoyed. Waiting for me to get pregnant couldn't be any easier for him than it had been for me. For the first time, it occurred to me— what if he thought *he* was the problem?

———

Half asleep with my back to the door, I stirred when Manning entered our bedroom, the dogs' nails clicking on the wood floor after him. He set something on the nightstand, slid between the sheets and up against my backside. "Lake," he murmured.

"Hmm?"

"I need you."

I turned to him. "What do you need, Great Bear?"

He rolled on top of me, pushing my sleepshirt to my waist and sliding his hand down the front of my underwear. "Kiss me."

I put an arm around his neck, gasping as he plunged one finger into me and then another. I lifted my mouth to his, and as soon as our lips touched, he turned frantic, finger fucking me until I was so wet I could hear it. He shoved down his pants, and I had only seconds to wrap my legs around him before he drove into me.

I made a squeak of surprise, and he paused, his breath warm on my cheek. "Lake."

Once I'd gotten over the initial shock of him, I exhaled. "I'm fine, Manning, just . . ."

"What, Birdy?"

"I love you. So much."

He drew his hips back. "And still less than I love you."

"Impossible," I whispered. "Take what you need."

He lifted onto his arms and did just that, fast and hard, until I'd slid to the top of the bed with the force of his thrusts. He stopped to put a pillow between me and the headboard, then grabbed the rail for leverage as he resumed fucking me. "You want a baby?" he growled at me.

I was high enough on him, raw and aroused enough to growl right back. "*Yes*."

"You're going to come with me, understand? Your tight motherfucking pussy's gonna squeeze every last drop out of me."

"Yes," I groaned, resigning my will, my heart, my body to him.

He didn't relent until I started to come apart, orgasming around him as he plunged to the hilt and came deep. He collapsed on top of me, a sign he was truly lost to the moment, since he normally worried about crushing me. Without words, because there really wasn't anything to say in those rawest moments, we each drifted to sleep.

I woke up alone in the middle of the night and looked over at the clock on his nightstand. I had to sit up to read it since he'd left a bottle of aspirin and water in the way. For my headache, I guessed. It was two in the morning and silent in the house.

The puppies slept soundlessly, but Blue was gone. I rubbed my eyes, sitting back against the headboard.

"You want a baby?"

I wasn't dense. Manning had probably known all along what was going on with me. This wasn't the same kind of obstacle we'd come up against in the past. Back then, we'd had a sliver of control over our destiny, and we'd taken that little bit and pushed it wide enough to make room for ourselves. This time, it was out of our hands. This was the circle of life, and I was being weeded out of the ground.

Did I want a baby? What the hell did he think? That if he fucked me hard enough, came deep enough, wanted it badly enough, *then* it would happen?

I got out of bed, put on my slippers and robe, and searched the house. When I'd checked the kitchen and den, I stopped at a closed door in the hallway. I hadn't been in what was supposed to have been a *temporary* office in months. We'd been so sure we'd get pregnant quickly and need the tiny room.

The porch light gave him away. I went out the front door and almost tripped over Blue resting at the top of the steps. I crouched down to pet her. Manning stood by the fire pit in his sweats, one hand in his hoodie pocket, the other delivering a cigarette to and from his mouth. He faced the house, staring forward, not seeming to notice me. Even from a distance I could see concern threading his brows.

He took his hand from his pocket to massage the bridge of his nose, then the back of his neck and shoulders. There was no question he was concerned about our future. Maybe he'd had a hunch all along that a baby wasn't in our cards but had been putting on a brave face for me. He was such a good man. The *best* man. Always putting me first, making sure I was happy. I wanted nothing more than to thank him for that by making him a father. By showing him the kind of mother I could be to his children. Was there any better way to express how deeply I loved him? And if I couldn't, would I be enough for him as I was?

Forever?

No. How could I be? No matter how much Manning loved me, and he couldn't any more than he already did, it would never compare to the love a parent has for his child. Although not bearing my own children was proving painful to come to terms with, not being able to give that to Manning was the real knife in my gut.

I wanted to go to him, but tears built at the base of my throat. If he treated me the way he did every day—with love and respect and endless affection—I'd break down and tell him everything.

Manning blinked and shifted his gaze, as if waking from a dream. "Everything okay?" he asked me.

I pulled my robe more tightly around me, suddenly noticing the cold night air on my bare legs. "I woke up, and you weren't there."

He showed me his cigarette. "I needed one."

I descended the steps and crossed the lawn to him. The act of walking, of moving, cleared the ever-present haunting thoughts from my head and extinguished any urge to cry. He'd *almost* quit this shit, but now he was back at it, using nicotine to calm his thoughts when I had to live with the turmoil of my own. That didn't seem fair. I glared at the cigarette. "Why?"

He flicked ash into the grass and shook his head. "Got a lot on my mind."

"And I don't?" Guilt gnawed at me, an overwhelming sense of inadequacy prickling its way up my chest, a kind of emotional heartburn. Why didn't he just come out and admit there was a problem? Why didn't he ask me to go to a doctor, to do *something*, to get confirmation that we were fucked? "I don't understand why you can't quit," I said. "Why do you need this? Why do you put yourself at risk every fucking day—every *night?*"

"I don't smoke every night."

"Really? This isn't the first time I've woken up and found you gone. You'd rather spend your time out here killing yourself than in a warm bed next to your wife?"

He studied the cigarette a moment, then looked back at me. "I've had this habit since the day you met me, Lake."

"Stupid me. I always thought I could love you enough that you'd stop killing yourself for me. I used to think Tiffany was so weak for letting you smoke."

"I told you, nobody makes me do what I don't want to. Everything I do for you, I do because I want to. Because I love you. This," he said, holding up the smoke, "is for me."

"Why?"

"Because it feels good."

"And because it's the only thing that brings you peace. You have so much on your mind that you have to drug yourself." Blue appeared at my side as I balled my hands into fists. "You told me in the truck I couldn't get away with not telling you what was wrong, but you keep stuff from me."

"I don't," he said calmly. "I have in the past, yes, but not anymore. I respect you too much. You want to know what's on my mind? I'll tell you. Babies."

My heart sank. I curled my toes in my slippers and muttered, "I knew it."

"They cost money. As do dogs. Happy as I am running my own business, I have no guarantees. There's no employer paying my wages or providing us health coverage or contributing to my 401k. I'm that employer. It's on me."

"Money?" I asked, my mind reeling to catch up. "You're worried about money?"

"Fuck yes I am."

Blue whimpered the way she sometimes did when one of us cursed.

"You can't honestly tell me it's never crossed your mind that my business might dry up and go away tomorrow," he said. "And then what? What happens when we have a small human to take care of?"

I started to laugh. I couldn't help it. Manning was worried about supporting a family he probably wouldn't have. "I *can* honestly say that has never crossed my mind. Your business isn't going to collapse for no reason, but if it does, I make a good salary. I've got great healthcare. You don't *have* to be the breadwinner."

He shook his head, cigarette between his lips as he pulled up his sagging sweatpants. "I've always wanted to take care of my family, since the day you met me. Don't act so surprised."

"I've never met anybody more responsible with money than you," I said. "You've been saving since you were fifteen. You even survived the market crash."

"I might not've if I'd hired on help a few months earlier like your dad wanted me to." He gestured at the workshop behind the house. "If my business fails, I fail anyone who works for me. They have families, too."

I hadn't even realized all this was running through his mind. He'd assured me over and over I could talk to him about anything bothering me, but had he not felt I'd reciprocate? "I wouldn't trust *my* family with anyone else," I said. "I have every faith we'll be fine, and you know why? Because you've never given me a reason to feel otherwise."

He looked to the sky. "Lake, if I love my child anywhere near as much as I did my sister, and obviously, that'll be the case . . . I don't know." With his eyes up, I watched his throat ripple as he swallowed. "I'd never survive losing them . . . or you."

I pulled on his arm to get him to look at me, but he wouldn't. "Manning?" I asked.

"Yeah, Birdy."

"Nothing's going to happen to me. I promise."

Without moving his head, he let his eyes drop to mine. "You don't know that. I want a guarantee that I can fix the bad things that might lie ahead of us. Money is the best way to do that."

I covered my mouth at the sad irony. In vitro fertilization and adoption were options, and neither was cheap—but all the money in the world wouldn't *guarantee* a baby of our own.

"Go inside," he said when I shivered. "You're not wearing enough clothing to be out here."

I didn't know what to say. How to tell him the truth. I focused on the orange tip of his cigarette as it flared with his next drag. "You can't tell me what to do."

"I'm not," he said, exhaling. "I'm looking out for you. I don't want you to get sick."

"That's because you care about me, and I care about *you*, too." I tried to snatch the smoke from him, but he held it over his head.

"What are you doing?" he asked.

"Put it out, Manning." Warmth rose to my cheeks as he stood there defying me. I'd had enough of the disgusting habit. "I'm serious."

"I'll come inside in a sec. I'm almost done."

"Maybe *that*," I snapped, pointing at the cancer stick in his hand, "is why we can't have babies. Did you ever think of that?"

He jerked back as if I'd suddenly sprouted a second head. "*What?*"

"In case you haven't noticed," I said, raising my voice, "*I'm—not—pregnant.* And after sixteen months of trying, it's time to stop pretending this isn't real."

Manning had frozen in place. Slowly, he squatted to put out his cigarette. "Nobody's pretending."

"Aren't you?" I asked. "Don't lie and say you haven't noticed how long it's taking."

"I've noticed, yeah, but I just figured it takes us a little longer than others. We have time."

"You don't get it," I said, tears overwhelming me. "I *can't* get pregnant."

"We don't know—"

"I do. I do know. I've been to the doctor and she did an exam, and she thinks I'm . . ."

He stared up at me, his eyes wide. "You're what?"

"Infertile."

I looked down at him, at the cigarette butt pinched between his fingers. It was a fucked-up thing to blurt out. It was even more fucked up to blame him for this when I knew it wasn't his fault. He'd been nothing but supportive and didn't deserve to be ambushed. I wasn't sure why I'd done it, but I got a strong sense of satisfaction when he ashed out the cigarette. Maybe that was why I'd suddenly needed him to know—to put a stop to his worrying.

"When was this?" he asked.

"Does it matter?" I asked, sniffling.

"Yes."

"January."

"And you never thought to mention it?" he asked. "That was months ago."

"Of course I did. It's all I've been able to think about. I didn't know how to tell you, though. I was scared—"

"No shit, Lake," he said, standing. "That's why you should've told me."

"That's not the point."

"Yes it is. How am I supposed to be here for you if you shut me out?"

He reached for me, but I stepped back. If he held me now, I'd never get the rest of it out. "I wanted to get a second opinion first," I said. "I didn't want you to hurt the way I'm hurting unless I knew for absolute sure." I inhaled a shaky breath. "But when everyone around me is getting knocked up out of nowhere—Tiffany, Val, Blue—"

"Blue's a *dog*, Lake."

"She wasn't supposed to get pregnant, and neither was Val. But I *am*. We deserve this."

"Do you have any idea what it's like inside my head?" He tapped his temple, his jaw tight. "I think about you all the time. I've told you before, I want every one of your thoughts."

I'd already heard that same speech once today. Manning needed to know everything about anything to do with me—that was no surprise. "Then you can thank Corbin for convincing me to talk to you."

"Corbin?" he asked. "What the fuck does he have to do with this?"

"Nothing." I didn't want to keep my conversation with him from Manning, but as soon as I said it, I realized I'd made it sound as if I'd said all these things to Corbin first. "I didn't tell him any details, just that you and I have been trying—"

"You talked to him about this?"

"I'm saying no, I didn't." It wasn't exactly a lie, but it felt like one. I bit my bottom lip. "Not really.

When he saw how I reacted to Val's news, he put two and two together and guessed we were having trouble."

Manning shoved his hands in the pockets of his hoodie. "Lake, you don't ever talk to anybody but me about something like this, especially not him. Especially not *before* you talk to me."

"I didn't discuss it with him," I said, exasperated. "We talked about getting pregnant, that's all."

"And you told him we were having trouble? Before you and I have even opened the door to that conversation?"

I thought of how tense I'd been watching Manning and Tiffany talk alone. I wrapped my arms around myself. "I guess."

"It's none of his goddamn business."

"He was trying to *help*. For God's sake, he was on your side. You act like he's trying to come between us, something I thought we'd moved past."

He snorted, pulling a pack from his pocket. "I could give a fuck about him. He's no threat to what you and I have." He slid out another cigarette. "But when we're talking about the most important thing in our lives, *I* come first. *You* come first. That's it."

"But—"

"You have no argument here, Lake. You're in the wrong."

Frustration boiled up in me so fast, my chin trembled. So *what* if I was wrong? Didn't I have the right to be? To get upset for no reason? To know I'd messed up and not want to acknowledge it? I might be *infertile*. I was trying to tell Manning this was the end of a future we'd counted on.

I pinched my robe closed at the neck. "Enjoy your fucking cigarette," I said as I turned back for the house.

17

With each step away from Manning, my chest stuttered with the threat of tears. I headed toward our bedroom, but I knew he wouldn't be far behind. I needed a minute alone, so instead, I ducked into the one room he'd be least likely to look for me.

The "temporary" office that had ended up staying for years.

We'd never wanted to put much effort into it, assuming it'd one day move to a more permanent spot in the house. There was just a desk, a small filing cabinet, and a computer. These days, I only came in to clean.

I rested my back against the door and looked around what might as well have been an empty room. It was small, just big enough to take a baby through the toddler years before we moved him or her into the next room.

I put my hands over my mouth and sobbed into them, hoping Manning wouldn't hear. I'd expected him to be devastated about my news, but instead he'd focused more on the fact that I'd kept it from him. I understood why that upset him, especially since I'd opened up to Corbin of all people, but there was a chance *we might not have children*. We weren't getting the family I'd promised him and myself. *That* was a reason to be upset. *That* was why he should've been smoking all along. His money concerns hadn't even scratched the surface of what we were about to face.

I walked to the middle of the room. The moon lit up the dark, and even as my eyes blurred with tears, I couldn't keep my imagination from filling in the blanks around me. Picturing the space as a nursery was easy because I'd done it many times over the years. We'd paint the walls. Put a crib in the corner by the window, because Manning had spent part of his life without one and was obsessed with making sure every room had plenty of light. My parents would've filled the room with gifts, and Manning and I would've been in here all hours of the night, the baby in my arms or his as we rocked our son or daughter to sleep.

Manning had asked if I'd thought of names—*of course* I fucking had.

He made me feel like a princess. His love turned me invincible, setting the world at my fingertips. Or so I'd thought. I'd taken that for granted, and now it was time to crash and burn.

The door opened behind me. I didn't *need* to hide my crying from Manning, but I hated for him to see me this way. He took my tears as hard as possible. They hurt him in a real way, and over the years, he'd bent over backward to make them stop. Like the time right after I'd moved in and found a fallen baby bird out back. He'd helped me put it in a shoebox—trying to be as delicate as he could with his enormous, fumbling hands—and driven us to the animal hospital. Another time, I'd come home from school and tearfully relayed a seminar about the declining elephant population, and he'd promised to take me to Africa one day to see them in person. Then one winter when I'd been miserably sick and crying for no reason, and he'd held me, even knowing I was contagious.

Tonight was no different. The more I held back, the harder my body shook. Manning came into the room and turned me by my shoulders, pulling me into his arms. I didn't stand a chance. Pressed against him, surrounded by his warmth and comfort, I released all the pain I'd been trying to shield him from the past couple months and beyond.

"Birdy," he whispered into my hair. "Please don't cry."

"I can't handle this," I told him. "I can't do it on my own."

"You *can* do it. You can handle this." He squeezed me so tightly, for a moment, I couldn't breathe. "But you never, ever have to do it on your own. I'll always be here."

"I'm so sorry," I sobbed into his hoodie.

"What for?" he asked. "This isn't your fault."

"I should've come to you right away. We're supposed to be a team, and I broke that promise."

"I get that you were scared," he said, rubbing my back, "but you have to understand. I never want to be shut out, and I sure as hell don't want anyone else to be let in."

"I know," I said, looking up at him. "I won't do it again. But Manning, did you hear what I said out there?"

He moved a couple strands of my hair off my wet cheek. "I heard."

"What if this is my fault?"

"It's not."

"But I took that pill. In New York, after I left your hotel room, I took the morning-after pill. What if I hadn't? What if that'd been my chance to give us a baby?"

He peeled me back by my shoulders, shaking me a little as he looked into my eyes. "You *know* it doesn't work like that. We don't deserve this because you did what you had to do years ago."

"I promised you so much—children, a family, a future—and now I don't think I can give it to you."

"You *are* my family." He slapped the back of his shoulder. "I burned you, my star, right here on my fucking skin. You have already given me the world. The goddamn universe."

I shook my head, and my voice broke as I said, "Not without a baby."

"Lake, listen to me carefully. I love you so fucking much. You hear me? As long as I've had you, it has never once crossed my mind that my life isn't complete. All I want is what you want. If you want a baby, we'll have a baby. If you want a litter of mutts, then lucky us—we've already had our first one."

"I want a *baby*," I said, "with you."

He inhaled through his nose, and for a terrifying moment, I thought he might break down along with me. Instead, his expression cleared. "What'd the doctor say? What's the issue?"

"She thinks I have endometriosis, but she won't know for sure until she performs a laparoscopy."

"What is that?" he asked. "I don't know any of those terms."

"I don't even understand it myself. I was in shock when she told me."

"I should've been there."

I tried to steady my voice so I wouldn't scare him any more than he already looked. "Endometriosis is a disease that causes my uterine tissue to . . . well, I guess the tissue has sort of blockaded one of my fallopian tubes. Literally keeping your sperm and my egg apart. And there are cysts on my ovaries—"

"Jesus, Lake." He released me to run a hand through his hair, leaving it sticking up. "You've known this for months?"

"It sounds more painful than it is."

"But is it?" His face fell as he nearly whispered, "Are you in pain?"

I wanted to tell him no, not ever—as far as my protective bear was concerned, I was perpetually floating on cloud nine. But I also wanted to be honest. "Some women have a lot of pain," I said. "I'm lucky that I don't. It's only slightly more severe around my periods."

"Fuck." He ran his hand down his face, the way he did when his gears were turning. "All right," he said. "We'll handle this. When's your next appointment?"

"I haven't made it."

I hadn't realized I'd crossed my arms over my stomach until he took my hand. "We need to, baby. No question."

"My gynecologist wants to do a laparoscopy—it's minimally invasive surgery. It'll tell us more."

"Surgery," he repeated.

"It'll most likely be outpatient and I'll recover within a couple days," I reassured him, the memory of my visit returning. I was pretty certain I'd only begun to regain composure because I couldn't quite believe we were having this conversation.

"We'll call her to schedule in the morning," he said. "Did she mention our options?"

"Options?" I asked. "There are no options. We just have to keep trying."

"IVF?" he asked. "Is that what people do next in our situation?"

Breaking this news to Manning hadn't gone anything like how I'd imagined. I'd thought discussing our options would come much later. "What do you know about IVF?"

"Not much," he said, "but enough that it concerns me."

"I haven't really thought about it," I admitted. "I didn't think you'd be ready to hear any of this."

"Not crazy about the idea of involving drugs and needles and labs." He brought my hand to his mouth, kissing my palm. "After all, I vowed to protect every inch of this body. If it's what you want, I'll support it, but . . ."

I frowned, my cheeks tight with dried tears. "But what? The money?"

"No. This is why I work hard—to give us options. I don't want you to rule out adoption, though. There are babies and children out there who need the love of a good mom and dad."

I couldn't handle it. I started bawling all over again, shivering so hard that Manning had to bring me back into his embrace. He rubbed my back, shushing me, trying to calm me down. My tears weren't sad. They were shock—that Manning would even consider adoption, and so quickly. They were guilt—that I'd assumed he'd never be open to it. And they were relief—this wasn't a deal breaker for him, and I could finally start asking myself what I wanted. Maybe our destiny was to give another child a safe and loving home. Maybe a son or daughter whose parents wanted better for them—or who didn't deserve them, the way Manning's hadn't deserved him or Madison.

"You'd really be okay with that?" I blubbered.

The words must've been unintelligible in my state, but of course Manning understood me. "This is *our* life, Lake. We can do whatever we want. We've never followed the conventional path. If we aren't meant to have a biological child . . . I mean, I can't lie. Yeah, that's hard news to take. I know how much you want that. I do, too. But it isn't the end of the line for us. Not even close." He tilted my face up with his knuckle. "Even if we have to make the difficult decision that it's just going to be you and me for the rest of our lives, I'll continue thanking the heavens. Every day. Won't you?"

My muscles loosened, and I finally let myself melt in his strong arms. It would be easy not to believe him, or to go on doubting what we had, but deep down I knew the truth. Manning wouldn't lie to me about this. He was enough for me—why shouldn't I, alone, be enough for him, too? Any other blessings fate sent our way were only more reasons to be grateful.

"Every day," I agreed.

I let Manning hold me in a nursery that might never be. I wasn't sure how to be okay with that yet.

Tonight, I'd perch on my great bear's back and let him carry me around the universe until I was ready to open my wings again. We were two stars forever locked in a triangle that only seemed to hurt us. But at least we had each other. I didn't know how long it'd be until I was ready to soar, only that Manning would support me when I was—and that I'd one day find the strength to do it.

SUMMER TRIANGLE
FALL 2012

18

I slid my hand up Manning's shaft, palming the leathery knob. "Like this?" I asked.

Manning stared as I stroked his stick shift. "Nice try," he said.

"What do you mean?"

"Sex won't get you out of this." He nodded at my feet. "Now, release the clutch smoothly as you feed in throttle."

With a sigh, I made my fourth attempt in fifteen minutes to drive a stick shift. Manning's truck jerked back and forth before I hit the brake. "I suck at this," I said.

"You'll get the hang of it." He started in again on downshifting and *listening* to the engine and friction points. The sun shone through the windshield, showing the crow's feet around his eyes, the two lines that formed in his forehead whenever he spoke about something that mattered to him. Like driving a manual.

Maybe I wasn't getting the hang of it because I kept losing myself in how sexy Serious Manning could be.

"Got it?" he asked.

"Today is one of those beautiful fall days that're gone before you know it," I said.

He covered my hand with his, ignoring me. "Now, put it in first," he said, pushing the stick to the left and up, "and slowly release the clutch."

"The sun is shining; the temperature is that perfect place between warm and cool. Let's go out on the lake."

"All right," he said. "Drive us there."

I stuck out my tongue at him. We made it farther down our driveway this time, rattling over the gravel as the truck shuddered. But at the entrance to the street, I slammed on the brakes in a panic, vaulting us forward as we stalled.

He scratched his chin. "That was better, I guess . . ."

I put the truck in park and flopped over into his lap as my stomach somersaulted. "I'm getting carsick," I said. "Why do I have to learn this again?"

"Because I've gone all around town bragging about what a badass wife I have. She can move to New York City all by herself. She applied for a loan while working a full-time job, then started her own practice. She saves people's pets on a daily basis. But always in the back of my mind, I'm thinking, 'if only she could drive a manual.'"

I playfully pushed his chest. "Shut up."

"Ooph." He winced. "Easy, Sugar Ray."

I laughed at his faux-pained expression and at the absurd idea that I could hurt him. "Sugar Ray?"

"The boxer, not the band."

"You know they're from Newport Beach?" I asked. "Tiffany claims she almost made out with the lead singer."

"How does one *almost* make out?"

"Right?" I kicked my feet and giggled so hard that my eyes watered.

"What's so funny?" he asked.

"I honestly don't know," I said. "I feel loopy from all the jerking around."

He put a hand on my face, thumbing the apple of my cheek. "It's good to see you laugh."

It *felt* good to laugh. Not that Manning and I didn't have fun. We'd gone drunk bowling a few weeks before and had shut down the alley before we'd come home and made love on every surface of the house. *That* had been fun. Regardless, fate's dark cloud crept along with us, reminding us it wasn't far away.

After another year of trying to have a child, Manning and I had decided to begin the adoption process. We'd been through a successful homestudy with an agency last year and had just received our third rejection from another birth mother. It turned out Manning's past had hit us in the one place we hadn't expected it to. Having a felony record didn't exactly make us ideal candidates as parents.

As a last resort, we'd scheduled an appointment with my doctor to seriously discuss IVF.

I ran my fingers against the side of his scalp. His chest rumbled the way it sometimes did when I played with his hair. "*You* make me laugh," I said. "You're a good man, Manning."

He nodded. "Because of you."

I worried about what the rejections did to him since Manning had a history of beating himself up and blaming himself for things outside his control. Even though he'd remained optimistic, it was hard to forget all the strife he'd put us through thinking he didn't deserve me. And now others were telling him he didn't deserve *to be a father*. There was no way each rejection didn't kill him just a little inside. He acted brave, but for nights after each of those phone calls, he loved me a little harder, and held me closer as we slept.

"They don't know what they're missing," I said softly.

"I know. And I'm disappointed, because I really don't want you to go through IVF." He ran some of my hair through his palm, resting it over my breasts. "But it might be the only option left."

"We'll find our baby."

"And it'll be a lucky goddamn kid."

Hearing him say that, my heart swelled. He'd come a long way since the days when he'd never let himself believe he deserved anything at all. I was grateful he'd finally found his hope in us. I wrapped my hand around his wrist and brought his palm to my lips. "Yes it will."

"With a badass mom who can drive stick."

"Point taken," I said with a sigh. I grabbed the steering wheel to pull myself upright, but I sat forward too fast and a wave of nausea hit. Manning leaned in to kiss me as I covered my mouth and gagged.

"Jesus." He drew away. "Way to kill a guy's confidence."

Shaking my head, I opened my door and leaned over the side. My stomach heaved as I prepared to throw up.

Manning slid over to rub my back. "I thought you were kidding about feeling sick."

"I'm allergic to stick shift," I said to the gravel.

"Aw, Birdy." He massaged my shoulder from behind. "Since when do you get motion sickness?"

"I do sometimes. I told you about that one time as a kid when Tiffany took me on the pendulum carnival ride."

"Yeah, but lots of people throw up after that."

I eased into a sitting position when nothing came. "You think I'm faking to get out of learning to drive stick?"

He arched an eyebrow, teasing me. "I wouldn't put it past you—but no. I was thinking something else."

I scanned his face as I registered his meaning. Of course, it would've been my next thought if I ever left myself think it. I didn't, though. After *years* of nothing, there was no point jumping to such an unlikely conclusion. "It isn't anything but the car."

"You don't know that."

"We've been trying too long," I said, irritation creeping into my voice despite the fact that I'd just laughed until I'd cried. He and I had been through this before, most recently when I'd thought I'd missed my period, only to get it on the way home from buying a pregnancy test. "It's not going to happen out of the blue."

"Lake, honey. That's *exactly* how it happens." He took my hand, entwining our fingers. "Letting yourself want this, and hope for it, doesn't mean it has to be heartbreaking when it doesn't happen. It just means we have to keep pushing forward with all available methods. Not even for ourselves, but for the kid."

I stared through the windshield, past our mailbox with the fading Summer Triangle he'd painted in red, into the thicket of trees across the street. Part of why I hated taking pregnancy tests was because with each negative result, I was disappointing Manning. He'd remained hopeful, while I'd only become more jaded. It wasn't easy for me to wait for an outcome that never came, but over the years, I'd done a better job of mentally preparing myself. Manning seemed to think one day, the second pink line would magically appear.

"We talked about this when we started the adoption process," I said. "We were supposed to stop wishing for a biological child."

"Why can't I want both?" he asked. "It's not a crime to want this, Lake. You never lost hope in me, and look at us now." He squeezed my hand and put it back on the shift. "Wasn't it worth holding onto?"

I nodded with a sigh. It was just motion sickness—I didn't get it often, but like everyone else in the world, I'd had it enough in my life to know what it felt like. The way Manning smiled warmly at me, though, I couldn't help but give in. "All right. I'll try to be more optimistic."

"Think you can get us back up the driveway?"

"The sun might set before I do, but I'll give it a go."

After another twenty minutes on our own private carnival ride, I managed to get the car in front of the garage before I shut off the engine and jumped out.

A few steps toward the house, the dogs came running out to meet us. As I squatted to say hi to Altair, I detoured to vomit on the lawn.

"Shit." Manning came up behind me as Vega tried to lick my face. "No, Vega," he said, pulling her away by her collar. "Go in the house."

"I'm fine," I said.

"I was talking to the dogs." He waited until I stood, then put an arm around my waist. "But we better get you on the couch, too. I'll find something for your stomach."

Inside, Manning put chicken soup on the stove as I went to our bedroom. Still queasy, I put a small trashcan by the bed and pulled my hair into a ponytail. As I brushed my teeth, I paced the bathroom, trying to ignore my thoughts.

That pregnancy test I'd bought but never used? It was still in a drawer under my sink. Even though I'd hidden it in the back, I accidentally came across it now and then, and each time, my heart dropped. If nothing else, peeing on the thing and tossing it would be a good way to get rid of it. I rinsed my mouth, swiped the test from the drawer, and unwrapped it on my way to the toilet. Even though I'd used this brand a few times, my nerves always got the better of me. I read the instructions to calm myself.

I was supposed to put the stick in a cup of urine—my first urine of the day—but it didn't matter. It wasn't going to be positive. I peed directly on it, then set it on the bathroom counter.

As soon as I'd perched on the edge of our tub, Manning leaned into the bathroom. "Soup's ready. Want me to go get you something from the drugstore?"

"No."

"I don't mean a pregnancy test. If you're coming down with something, I can pick up some . . ." He paused at the look on my face. "What's wrong? Did you puke again?"

"No."

"You look like you're about to pass out, Lake. Why aren't you in bed?"

True, my stomach was still queasy, but I doubted that was the reason I looked sick. "I took it," I said. "The test."

With a glance at the stick on the counter, *he* started to look a little pale. "Oh."

"I just thought maybe—"

"You don't have to explain." Manning crossed the bathroom and came to sit next to me. I hadn't realized I was gripping the lip of the tub until he put his hand over mine. "How do you feel?"

"Better with you here," I said.

He kissed my temple, pausing there as he inhaled. "I'm proud of you. No matter what it says, it's okay to want this."

"Will you look for me?" I asked.

"Sure." He stood and took a few steps toward the counter, where he picked up the stick.

Seconds ticked by. "Anything?" I asked.

"Not yet."

"Let's forget it." My heart pounded. I could see his expression in the mirror, and I didn't want to watch it turn from expectant to disappointed. I got up. "I don't want to know."

"Lake," he said, a warning should I try to leave.

I got behind him, hiding from whatever face he was about to make. That wasn't enough, so I pulled up his t-shirt, stuck my head under first, and drew it down around me.

"What're you doing?" he asked.

"Just pretend I'm not here." I hugged him from behind—in the dark, where I could hold onto the one thing that mattered—him. My Manning. My first love. My husband. The one thing that wouldn't disappoint me, leave me, hurt me. I wanted more, but I didn't *need* it. Emotionally, he was enough for me. *Physically*, he was big enough, too, a safe space for me to burrow into. I could've stayed pressed against his warm back forever. "I don't want to know," I repeated, my lips on his skin.

He covered my arm, lacing our hands through his shirt.

From his silence, I had my answer.

We made love nearly every day. It was the best we could do to move the stars. Maybe, this time, they simply refused to budge.

Manning's torso expanded under me as he breathed. I traced the thin black triangle on his shoulder, touching each star. He didn't know how to tell me the test was negative, but we'd been through this before.

"It's okay," I said. It wasn't really okay, but I needed Manning to believe I could handle this. *I* needed to know I could, or else I'd give up on completing our family altogether. "Take me to the couch, Great Bear. You can carry me and put blankets over me and feed me soup. You're so good at taking care of me."

"It's positive."

"I know," I said before he'd even gotten the words out—except *what*? My heart dropped to my feet, and I froze, my fingertip between stars. I didn't move an inch, not even to breathe, in case I might disrupt the delicate synergy of a moment fate had decided to bestow on us. "*Positive?*" I asked, trying out the word.

"There are pink lines. Two of them. One is kind of faint, but . . . that's positive?" He knew it was, we'd done this often enough, but it came out sounding like a question anyway.

I excavated myself from inside his shirt, pushing back strands of my hair as they went wild with static. "Are you sure?" I took the test from him. Even with the positive result in front of me, I shook my head. "It can't be right."

"Why not?"

The emotion in his voice made me look up. His clenched jaw and big brown eyes undid me. I didn't want to let myself think this could be true, but Manning already believed it.

I closed my eyes. It was too early to get excited. There was a chance the test was faulty. I felt behind me for the tub so I could sit again. An unbidden tear slid down my cheek. "Manning . . ."

He kneeled in front of me. "I know."

I shook my head. "I'm scared."

"I'm not going to tell you not to be," he said, taking my waist. "I'm not going to promise everything'll be all right."

"I don't need you to." I opened my eyes and put my hands on his shoulders. "But I can't flip on my excitement like a switch. I need time to absorb this."

"I understand." He ran a thumb up the center of my tummy, and I shivered. "First thing Monday, I'll make us a doctor's appointment."

I tried to focus on his warm eyes that didn't judge or dismiss my fears. On his familiarly briny, masculine smell. On the way all ten of his fingers loosened on me, as if he'd just realized what was growing beneath them. Because my gut told me I *was* growing. In that moment, I couldn't believe I'd ever doubted it. "There's a baby in there," I whispered.

He pinched the inside corners of his eyes. I still hadn't ever seen him cry—he'd only come close a handful of times, like when opening up about his sister's drowning, or the time in New York when I'd forced him to say goodbye, and then when we'd exchanged vows.

"I'm sorry," he said as a few tears tracked down his cheeks.

"Why?" I asked, taking his face in my hands.

"I want to be strong for you."

"You are, baby." I kissed his resilient face, the lip that had been scarred and nose that'd been broken defending my honor. The gray hairs that'd started to shade his stubble, the lines that hadn't been there even five years ago, and the features that had, like the dent in his chin. No matter how much we'd been through, good or bad, his soda-pop brown eyes held the same intensity they had back then. I kissed the face his son or daughter would look up to for the first time months from now. To them, he'd be as high in the sky and as important as the sun.

"I love you, father of my child," I said.

"I love you, too," he said, his voice *'so deep, it gave me goosebumps on the inside, if that was even possible.'*

I smiled, remembering how painfully naïve and awed I'd been that first day we'd met on the construction lot nineteen years earlier. Squinting up at him like he was too bright.

We had grown and changed, laughed and hurt—and loved each other through all of it. I was a woman now, but maybe it wasn't so bad to still be that girl, too—my world warmed and given life by the sun.

19

I'd been so eager to get knocked up that I hadn't stopped to consider timing. Now, eight months and two weeks in, I wished I'd thought it through. Sex should've been off the table during any months that might result in a summer pregnancy.

"Hand me that," I said to Val, gesturing between us. "Hurry up."

The terrified look on her face only annoyed me more. "What are you pointing at?" she asked.

"Your flip-flop."

She and Tiff exchanged a glance that probably meant to ask if I was insane, but I didn't care. She took off her shoe and gave it to me. I started fanning myself. "Manning's house is a million fucking degrees."

"Suddenly it's Manning's house?" Val asked. "Not yours?"

"I never signed up to live in a sauna."

"It's really not that bad," Tiffany said. "But I know when I was pregnant—"

"It's *not* because I'm pregnant," I said. "It's the middle of June and Big Bear is experiencing an *extreme* heat wave."

"It's eighty-five degrees out . . ."

"Lake is right," Kara said, nodding at me with a soft smile. I'd gotten to know Henry's daughter better since my wedding, but I wasn't as close with her as I was with most of the girls in the room. "Hopefully Manning will get the A.C. fixed soon."

"Thank you, *Kara*," I said.

The flip-flop wasn't cutting it. I tossed it aside, looking for a paper plate, a magazine, an igloo to crawl into—anything. I rocked forward as best I could, stretching for the diaper tree on the coffee table, but in my enormous state, I couldn't get to it. "Someone hand me one of those."

"But it's arranged so pretty," said Piper, a friend from my veterinary program.

Kara moved the tree to the floor next my chair. A chair they'd made me sit in to put me on display.

I pulled a diaper out and relaxed back in my seat, waving it over my clammy face and neck. "That's better. Now what?"

"Well," Val said slowly, "I had this game planned."

"Great," I said. "I love games. Let's have some fun."

It was only then I noticed how quiet the room was. Val had not only organized me a baby shower, but she'd gone out of her way to invite people from coast to coast. Classmates, friends, and relatives had come from Los Angeles and Pomona, and even Roger had flown in from New York to be here— although, I suspected he was really in California to troll the West Hollywood summer scene. A few of the girls hadn't made the wedding, and they were floored by the house—I would have to tell Manning when I saw him, assuming I didn't die of heatstroke.

We'd all been having a nice time until the brand-new air conditioning unit had gone out. Luckily, Manning had been hiding out with the dogs in his workshop during the party and had jumped into action.

I made a hurry-up motion with my hand. "What's the game?"

"It's called Dirty Diapers," Val rushed out.

"We played it at my shower, and you won, remember?" Tiffany added. "Val and I thought it would be fun. We smash melted chocolate bars into diapers, then pass them around for everyone to guess which candy it is."

"Like poop?" I asked.

"Yes?" Val said.

"Is that a question?" I asked.

"We don't have to do it." Val smoothed her skirt over her thighs. Bless her, she'd worn a floral pattern for today. It was the most mom-like outfit I'd seen her in since she'd had Ella. "There's another game where we get out a measuring tape and guess the circumference of your belly . . ."

Was she serious? I looked like a hot air balloon—I didn't need confirmation I was *actually* the size of one. Sweat dripped from my under-boobs down my stomach. I pushed my damp hair behind my ear and shifted in an attempt to dislodge the underwear wedged up my ass.

Roger winced. "I don't think measuring anything is such a good idea . . ."

"Me neither," I agreed. "I don't remember the poop game, but I also forgot my niece's birthday last week and nearly had a panic attack trying to get a present in the mail the day before."

Tiffany pouted. "You forgot Coco's birthday?"

"Yes, and I also forgot you were sitting there," I said. "Give me a break. Pregnancy brain is a *real* thing."

Everyone laughed nervously. Val stood. "You know, I think I hear Ella crying in the playroom."

Tiffany grabbed her wrist. "I don't hear anything, but even if I did, that's why we hired a babysitter. I'm sure the kids are fine."

Slowly, Val sat. "All right."

If Val and Tiffany had formed an alliance, I must've really been a monster. I sighed. "I'm sorry.

I'm just so uncomfortable." I pointed around the room. "None of you said it would be this bad."

"It was the same for me, but I wasn't around people the final month," Piper said. "You're really brave."

"Brave, or ignorant?" I asked, shooting Val a look. "If I'd known, I wouldn't have agreed to do it so late."

Tiffany stood. "I definitely hear some weird noises coming from the playroom. I should probably check on Coco."

"Hey, what about the babysitter?" Val called after her, then muttered, "Traitor."

Manning came in the front door, wiping his brow with his t-shirt sleeve as he entered the living room. "Almost there, sweetheart," he said, smiling as I glared at him. Vega trailed after him the way she always did, barely noticing us. "I just need to play with the thermostat," he added.

All the women in the room turned, plus Roger. "Holy shit," he whispered.

Manning wore an old t-shirt with the sleeves ripped off. His biceps were as big as my head and covered in a sheen of sweat. For some reason, he was wearing a hardhat. I was pretty sure he hadn't put that thing on in years, which meant it was a hardhat with a purpose. I'd been yelling at him for two weeks straight—and he was definitely trying to remind me of the day we'd met so I'd remember why I loved him. It was working. The girls in the room were practically puddles of drool as they watched Manning stomp through the living room. My insides tightened with a sudden need to drag my husband into our bedroom. Or throw him down on the couch here, everyone else be damned. Had I always had a thing for dirty construction men, or did it only apply to Manning?

It didn't help that no matter my mood, or the last time Manning and I had been intimate, I'd been painfully aroused for months. Luckily, Manning had no qualms helping in that department, no matter how far along I was. Even though he regularly commented on my 'glow,' *he* was the radiant one. He couldn't have been in a better mood lately.

At least, for the most part . . .

There was, I'd noticed, something on his mind. He'd started leaving our bed in the middle of the night again, but this time, it wasn't to smoke—he'd quit the same day we'd gotten our pink lines. Now, he'd take his girl Vega on walks instead.

It wasn't money. His company had been steadily growing each year—he'd never even had time to pursue contracting like he'd planned—and I'd paid off my student loans a while back. My practice had opened right as the town's most popular vet had retired, giving me plenty of business.

All I could guess was that he was nervous about the birth, but he seemed fine whenever it came up. He'd read enough books on the subject that he could probably deliver the baby himself.

"Sorry, ladies," Manning said on his way to the hallway thermostat, furrowing his brows at all of us as we stared. "Pretend I'm not here."

Nobody looked away. Not even Val. She was not only my best friend, but she'd always hated Manning just a *little* bit. At the moment, she looked as if she were ready to ditch Corbin for him. We all followed him with our eyes until he'd disappeared into the hall.

Piper turned back. "*That's* your husband?"

"Has he been working out more than usual?" Val asked.

Kara shook her head with a dreamy sigh. "He's always been like that . . . so *Manning*."

I breathed through my nose. Basically, at forty-three, Manning looked better than ever. And I was an obese pig. "Maybe we should end the party early."

"No," some of them wailed.

Piper stuck out her bottom lip. "You haven't even opened your presents."

As if heaven itself had taken pity on me, the house shuddered ominously and the air conditioning kicked on. "Oh, thank *God*," I said.

Our landline rang, and Manning walked back through the living room toward the kitchen, Vega once again glued to his heels. "No, thank *me*," he said.

I narrowed my eyes on his tight, jean-clad ass. *Trust me, I will later.*

When I broke from my trance, everyone was staring at me. "Did I say that aloud?"

"Get it, girl," Roger said, winking at me.

"Don't worry," Kara added. "I was super . . . excited . . . during my first pregnancy."

"I wasn't," Val said. "I practically moved Corbin into a hotel until it was over, he was so annoying." She smiled a little. "In a sweet way, though."

"Robby, too," Tiffany said, reentering the room. "I hated him, except when I was horny."

"Same here," Val agreed.

Ugh. The thought of Tiffany and Robby or Val and Corbin or basically anyone in this room having sex was even less appetizing to me than chocolate shit in a diaper. Manning, on the other hand—I could've eaten him up like a slice of French Silk pie. Literally. I was so hungry.

I stood. "I'll be right back."

In the kitchen, Manning sat on a stool, his elbows planted on the island next to his hardhat as he rubbed a hand over his messy hair. By the distant look on his face, I'd caught him zoning out—and it wasn't the first time lately.

"Hey," I said. Vega blinked at me from where she lay by the kitchen table. "Who was on the phone?"

"Nobody." He straightened up. "I'm sorry about the air conditioning."

"It's okay." I smiled sweetly while I threatened, "As long as it doesn't go out again."

He held an arm open to me. "Come over here."

"No. I'm disgusting from sweating all afternoon. I need a cold shower and a nap."

"Shower sounds good," he said, beckoning for me. "Can I at least get a kiss?"

"Why?" I crossed my arms as best I could over my balloon boobs. "I wish you would just go away until after the birth. I've never felt more unattractive."

"Aw, Lake." He chuckled. "My love. My wife. You're lit from within. You must know you're as beautiful as ever, and that I've never loved you more."

My irritation fizzled into tears. I covered my face. "I know you're only saying that to make me feel better."

"Birdy, please." He got off the stool, came around the island—he had to get behind me to touch me, my stomach was so big—and moved my limp curls off my neck. "You're carrying my child. How many times do I need to tell you how sexy that is to me?"

I sighed as my skin cooled. "That feels nice."

"Why don't you put your hair up?" he asked. "Or at least change into a tank top?"

"I wouldn't subject my friends to that."

He raked my hair away from my face, holding it off my shoulders. "You know, you were making some . . . noises . . . while you slept last night."

"I *slept* last night?"

He laughed, but only for a second, his voice turning serious as he lowered his hand over the crotch of my jeans. How he could reach that far, I had no idea. "I did an Internet search and guess what? Just like at thirty-three weeks, we're allowed to fuck at thirty-four."

"Are you sure?" I asked, skeptical. "You have the biggest dick I've ever seen."

"Lake, mine is the *only* dick you've ever seen."

"Of course," I said. I'd forgotten for a moment that Manning had rewritten history, removing any other 'mutt' who'd ever come 'sniffing around' as he liked to say.

"Some people even think," he added seductively, "it could induce labor."

"Oh, God," I moaned, resting my head back against his shoulder. "You're making me wet."

Manning licked and sucked my neck in a way that instantly made me shudder. "If your friends weren't in the next room, I'd take you in the shower and fuck you right now."

I turned around and sobbed into his chest. "Don't say that. I'm so horny."

He laughed, wrapping his arms around me. "I would. I'd do it. Except for the sex in the shower part. We can wait until after. I don't want you to slip."

"I'd bounce right off the floor."

"Hang on a *little* longer," he said. "As soon as they go, my sperm is going to ripen the hell out of your cervix and possibly stimulate birth."

"I've never been more turned on." I sniffled. "I can't believe you're hugging me right now. You must have the longest arms in history."

"Hey."

I looked up at him. "What?"

He turned me by my shoulders to face the double ovens, our reflection slightly distorted in the chrome and glass doors. "I know you're joking, but please tell me you know how exceptionally beautiful you are right now. If you don't, I haven't done a good enough job showing you."

My chin trembled. Again. "I'm sorry. I just don't feel like myself."

"Like the doctor said, you are perfectly within the size and weight you should be."

"For carrying a nine-and-a-half-pound baby— you forgot that part."

He grimaced. "I'm sorry. You shouldn't have fallen for a giant."

Soon enough, I'd hold a Manning-sized baby in my arms.

Manning's *son*. I wasn't sure I'd ever get to say that, and now I couldn't imagine our lives any other way than with a little boy, our third star.

I covered Manning's hands on my shoulders. "Yeah, poor me."

He released me with a pat on the butt. "You better get back to the party before everyone makes a break for it. I heard a little bit of my moody bitch in there."

With a reluctant sigh, I started to leave the kitchen, then paused to look back at him. "You never said who was on the phone."

He hesitated. "We can talk about it after."

"After the shower?"

"After the birth."

I turned around, blinking at him. "All right, Sutter. Out with it."

"With what?"

"Whatever's been going on the past couple months that you're not telling me."

Vega rolled onto her side and groaned, as if to say "here we go."

"It's a sad story," he said, sniffing as he peeked into a Tupperware of blue sugar cookies on the island. "A problem I don't know how to fix, and trust me—it'll only make you cry."

"I won't cry, I promise." I tried to look serious, but the truth was, I routinely felt on the verge of tears. I turned to get a glass from a cupboard so he wouldn't see me falter, and also because my mouth was minutes away from shriveling into a desert.

"If you insist." As I opened the freezer, he checked through the doorway to ensure nobody was listening. "It was Cheryl."

I paused while scooping ice into my glass. "From the adoption agency?"

"Yeah."

"Why? They know we're pregnant."

"She and I have kept in touch the past couple months. She'd called back in March with this case—a boy she thought we could help with, and you wouldn't believe this kid's story . . ." He scratched his jaw, leaning on the island. "It hit a little close to home for me, so I asked her to keep me updated."

"Close to home?" I could tell by the look on his face this was serious. I braced myself with a long drink of water. I would've considered pouring the rest over my head if I didn't need to be presentable a little longer. I set down the glass, took a breath, and steadied myself against the island opposite him. "Okay. Who is he?"

"Nine-year-old boy who's, as of a few months ago, an orphan."

"Oh, poor baby," I said, pressing my palm to my heart. "What happened to his parents?"

"His mom passed after he was born."

"And his dad?"

"Dead. The boy killed him—"

"*What?*" I asked so sharply, Vega raised her head.

"Let me finish." He tapped a finger on the island's surface. "The kid shot his dad *while protecting his eleven-year-old sister* from what Cheryl said could've been a fatal beating."

I dropped my jaw. Now I understood why it hit close to home. Manning, too, had intervened with his father to protect his sister. Unfortunately, it hadn't resulted quite the same way. "I can't believe that."

"Apparently, the kid knew where his dad kept his gun and when push came to shove, he just . . . snapped."

"He didn't snap. He *saved* her." *Snapped* was a word Manning used in reference to his dad's temper.

285

I knew that possibility scared him, in himself and in others, but this wasn't the same. "And now the boy's alone? What about the sister?"

"Relatives took her in. This is the worst part— they don't want anything to do with him."

The hair on my skin prickled. For the first time in recent history, sad news didn't actually make me want to cry. It made my already warm face heat with a familiar sense of frustration for a boy who'd been wronged. A familiar sense of *injustice*. For the kid, and for my Manning, an innocent man who'd had enough experience being unfairly defined by his criminal past. "Wow," I said, my heart racing. "Where is he now?"

"A group home, but Cheryl's worried there are bad influences there."

"How worried?" I asked.

He blew out a sigh. "Enough to call on a Sunday to see if I'd found anyone who could . . . help."

"Help," I repeated. "As in, adopt? Is that why she called us in the first place?"

"She knows my history with Madison and my dad, plus the fact that we've been rejected a few times." He pushed off the island, straightening his back. "All that considered, I guess she thought we'd be a good fit for the boy."

It was an eerily similar situation to what Manning had been through—and yet completely different. Manning had survived it the best he could've because of the family around him willing to help. I shook my head with disdain for the boy's relatives. "What'd you tell Cheryl?"

"That we're about to have a baby. That we'd never considered a kid that age. That we . . ." His jaw went taut. "It's just not the right time."

I didn't realize I was rubbing my stomach until I noticed Manning tracking my hand. "Bad timing," I murmured.

He went silent, staring at nothing on the ground. After a few seconds, he said, "I can't help but think of my sister."

Of course he couldn't help it. It was the first place my mind had gone as well. It hurt him to say no, but how could we help? We were about to have our hands full. Could we even take care of a young boy who'd survived more by nine than most did in a lifetime?

Manning was that boy. He'd also seen, done, and lost more than one person should ever have to—all by the age of fifteen. I got the unsettling feeling that I'd been here before. Helpless to change the situation. Disappointed in people and the system. Scared for a boy's future.

Only, I wasn't helpless now. Not like I'd been at sixteen. "He defended his sister," I said.

"I know. Caseworker said it doesn't matter. His relatives are treating him like a murderer when he'd had no other choice."

"Wouldn't you have done the same? If you'd known what your dad was doing to Maddy?"

His biceps tensed, his Adam's apple bobbing as he swallowed. I didn't need to hear his answer. I already knew what it was.

"He killed a grown man, Lake. We'll have a newborn in the house. Kids who go through trauma at that age can be fucked up."

"They can also turn out pretty great," I said with a look.

Manning's knuckles whitened as he gripped the counter, as if he were restraining himself. He was a protector, and he was also a good man. A champion for the underdog. I had no doubt he wanted to help, even though there were more than enough reasons not to. "I can tell you've given this a lot of thought," I said.

"A lot." He ran a hand through his hair. "What if my aunt hadn't been there to help? Or Henry? I would've either gone to juvie or a group home, and who knows where I'd be today."

I nodded. "Fate really has been on our side all along, Manning. Some things can never be explained, like your sister's death, but we're lucky." I placed my hands on my stomach as our son moved. Perhaps he was listening, throwing his opinion into the ring. "And the more we've fought, the stronger we've become. As individuals, and as a couple."

Manning came around the island and put his hands next to mine. "He's moving."

I nodded. "We have our baby and everything else we could ever ask for. And God knows we asked."

"Begged," he said with a faint smile.

I watched his expression closely. Despite the blissful look he wore whenever he felt the baby kick, Manning seemed suddenly tired, too—almost beaten down—for the first time since we'd found out we were pregnant. I supposed this sadness was what he'd been hiding from me on his late-night walks with Vega. Other than fatherhood, I tried to remember the last time Manning had wanted something. The last time he'd even asked me for anything. Besides the house and his business, he rarely did anything for himself.

He glanced up and caught me staring at him. "Lake," he said.

"What is it, Great Bear?" I asked. "Can't read your mind. You want something, you have to ask for it."

"It's not fair to you." He spread his hands on my tummy, brushing the tips of my middle fingers with his. "The next few months—years—are going to be chaos for us."

"But?"

"But I can't help feeling I'm turning my back on this kid, when I understand exactly what he's going through."

I waited for Manning to ask. This couldn't be for me—everything else he did, he did for me. Once the baby was born, Manning would be working overtime for both of us. If he wanted to adopt a nine-year-old boy, he had to say it aloud. He had to *need* it.

"What's his name?" I asked.

"Mateo. Mateo Alvarado."

"Mateo," I repeated. I formed a picture of him in my mind, a skinny, dark-haired kid weighed down by a gun. "Have you met him?"

He shook his head, removing his hands to cross his forearms over his chest. "I sent some things to Cheryl—boys' clothes and toiletries, that kind of stuff. He didn't even have a second pair of shoes. It doesn't feel like enough."

"Would *anything* feel like enough?" I asked.

"Only the obvious." He scrubbed his jaw, glancing out the window over the sink. He'd finished the stable long ago, but we'd shifted our focus right from dogs to babies and hadn't talked about getting a horse in a long time. Too much to handle—and yet here we were, discussing a nine-year-old boy.

Nine was terribly young—Maddy's age when she'd passed.

"What is it?" I prompted. "What's the obvious solution?"

He turned back to me, his eyes narrowed in thought. He struggled with whatever was running through his mind. "I want to help," he admitted. "I want to meet him."

Though I'd half-expected him to say it, it took my mind a moment to catch up. Manning and I could help financially from a distance. That meant there was really only one reason to meet Mateo. "And what if he's a good kid? Like you were?" I asked. I tried to

290

hide the emotion in my voice so Manning could make this decision on his own, but I suspected he saw through me. "What if he's being punished for doing the right thing?"

He hesitated. "Then I'm not sure I can stand by and let it happen. If that means adoption, then I guess that's what I want. Maybe it's selfish of me to ask that of you with everything we have going on."

I inhaled a deep breath. It was no small thing, what he was suggesting. I didn't know the right response, if one even existed, but I couldn't think of a time in recent history when Manning had been selfish. I'd tried to get him to be, actually, and he never was—which was how I knew this was important to him.

If I'd had the opportunity to save Manning years ago, either from his sister's death or from his prison sentence, I wouldn't have hesitated a moment. It was possible I wanted this, too—I wasn't sure. But Manning had asked for it, and I at least owed him my support until we learned more.

He cinched his brows, watching me. "What are you thinking?"

I held his gaze a few moments, his brown eyes torn but full of love. I'd fought hard for that love, for a permanent spot next to him in the universe, and to complete our little triangle. But triangles weren't the only shapes out there, not even in the sky. "I think we moved our stars, Manning," I said. "Maybe now, we help rearrange someone else's."

EPILOGUE
A HOT SUMMER DAY, 2018

I waited on the back porch, Mads balanced on my hip, while Henry tied his shoes. He had a very particular method of looping his bunny ears and would not be rushed—my son took after his father that way. Once satisfied, he got up from his knee and took my hand even though we were only going across the yard.

"Okay, Mommy," he said. "Let's go."

I took the kids down the steps and across the grass. Manning had opened all the doors and windows of his workshop, but neither he nor Mateo would've noticed a herd of elephants coming. Jimi Hendrix blared on the stereo, and Mateo played a hammer like an electric guitar while Manning sanded down a bedframe.

I whistled and waved until I got Manning's attention. He shut off the sander and lowered the volume before pushing his goggles onto his head.

As soon as Madison spotted her daddy, she reached for him, practically vaulting out of my arms. "She loves you more than me," I complained as he came over and took her from me.

"What can I say?" He bounced her to "Foxey Lady" and brushed her messy black curls from her face. "I have a way with the ladies."

I rolled my eyes. "It's fine," I said, bending down to squeeze Henry in a hug from behind. "Because this one's a momma's boy, aren't you, sweetheart?"

"Yes, Mom," he said as if I'd asked him to take out the trash. Henry was my serious little man—he looked just like Manning and acted as if he carried the world on his shoulders. I'd planned to call him Chuckie, the name my dad had gone by as a kid, but Henry had come out of the womb quiet and frowning, and I knew—he was *not* a Chuckie. Henry Charles Sutter it was, and even though my baby didn't cry on the day of his birth, both his godfather and grandfather had sure as hell shed tears of joy.

Mateo shuffled out of the workshop, cleaning his hands on a rag. At fourteen, he was taller, and almost skinnier, than me. "Since you're home today, are you making us lunch?" he asked.

"Hey." Manning nodded at him. "She's not your personal chef."

"Aren't I, though?" I asked. Nothing made me happier than feeding my family, and Manning knew it, but ever since we'd gone from the two of us to having young boys in the house, Manning had been even more of a stickler about showing me respect. No son of his would treat his woman as anything less than a queen.

"Sorry," Mateo said, bopping Mads on the nose as she giggled and tried to grab his finger.

"Actually, I am about to make lunch," I said. "We came out to take orders."

Manning removed the goggles on his head, tossing them on the nearest work table. "You even have to ask?"

"Two monster sandwiches?" I guessed.

Mateo nodded emphatically. "Yes, please. But you better make Dad one, too."

Manning eyed him. "I've taught you too well."

"I take it you boys are hungry?" I teased.

"Starved." Manning winked. "Why *are* you home today anyway?"

It was a fair question. I didn't normally close the practice for no apparent reason, but a small part of me had hoped Manning would puzzle the pieces together and remember today's anniversary. We'd recognized it on and off over time, but twenty-five years since we'd met seemed like a day to be home with him. "I just felt like having a family day," I said.

"That's it?" Mateo asked.

"Well . . ." I debated whether to remind Manning.

"Oh, almost forgot." Manning set down Mads and reached into his back pocket to pull out his red bandana.

I broke into a smile. He hadn't forgotten after all. "I can't believe you still have that thing."

"Same one," he said, knotting the bandana at the back of his head. "Did I ever tell you kids about the day I met your mom?"

Henry, standing in front of my legs, nodded. "Tell us again."

Mateo hoisted himself onto the work table. "It was a hot summer day," he began.

"She made me a killer sandwich," Manning said, ruffling Henry's hair, "and I was instantly in love."

"It didn't go quite that smoothly." I lowered my voice into storytelling mode and made tickle-monster hands at Mads as she sucked her thumb and hung onto her dad's leg. "We came up against some obstacles," I said.

Henry fixed his hair. "What's an obstacle?"

"Something in the way," Manning said.

"Or in our case," I said, glancing at Manning, "*someone*."

"The evil stepsister." Manning laughed at his joke, but I didn't. That was a real blemish on my fairytale if you asked me. Noticing my glare, his expression cleared. "Since I couldn't confess my feelings to your mom, who, by the way, was and *still is* extremely beautiful," Manning continued, "I told her the story of Altair and Vega."

296

"Summer Triangle," the boys said in unison.

"That's right." Manning pointed up, despite the fact that it was eighty degrees with clear blue skies. "And I made her a promise on the stars." Manning looked at me with his chocolatey brown eyes. "Remember?"

"No matter what, the story would only ever be about us," I said, puckering my lips at him with a loud *smooch*.

"Daddy kiss," Madison said, pulling on Manning's pant leg. He picked her up, pecking her pink cheeks all over.

Hearing their names, Altair and Vega had wandered from their usual grassy spots in the sun. Behind them followed the newest addition to our family. Blue had passed earlier in the year, and because I'd decided my life needed to have no less than three dogs or children, we'd adopted when I'd eventually felt ready.

In honor of Blue, who'd shared my eye color, Cola—a Saint Bernard Madison tried to ride on a daily basis—had been named for Manning and Henry's soda-pop brown eyes.

Not that she needed a makeshift pony. Her father had spoiled her with a horse for her second birthday, which gave me plenty of time to get used to the idea before she was ready to ride.

As Cola settled under Mateo's feet, I leaned against the table with him. It'd taken years before he'd started calling us Mom and Dad. In fact, from ages nine to twelve, Mateo had barely spoken beyond what was necessary. Manning had been the best kind of guardian for him—firm, honest, yet sensitive considering he and Mateo had experienced the same kind of pain—and Mateo had responded well. He'd been polite and helpful around the house, but it hadn't been until Manning had brought him out into the workshop that Mateo had begun to blossom. I'd been hesitant about him handling tools at his age, but Manning had assured me working with his hands had gotten him through some of his worst times.

Now, not only was Mateo growing into his limbs, but his personality, too. He liked all kinds of music— even Manning's "oldies" when he and his friends weren't listening to rap—and was learning to play electric guitar. He'd also signed up to be a counselor with Young Cubs thanks to Gary, who'd had a lot of experience with adopted kids at the Y and had treated Mateo as a nephew since the day he'd met him.

I'd worried not all relationships would form as easily. My white, conservative father's reaction to adoption in general had been a big concern, especially considering Mateo had come to us with a lot of issues and from a background similar to Manning's. But any reservations had flown out the window the moment I'd shared Mateo's test scores with my dad.

"He's smarter than you were at that age," my dad had said with renewed energy, "and you know what that means."

I'd feared I had.

"He's Trojan material," he'd exclaimed, and they'd been thick as thieves ever since. Mateo now had his sights set on USC, and he and my dad were already in cahoots about how much mileage they could squeeze out of his adoption, past, and Hispanic background for the admissions essay.

Lately, though, Manning and I had noticed that the older Mateo got, the more introspective he was becoming. He'd been a child when he'd shot his dad to protect his sister and he was now old enough to start asking harder questions. Even though he and Manning talked it through frequently, Mateo sometimes questioned whether there was some other way he could've handled the situation.

"Did you finish your homework?" I asked Mateo as he messed with the playlist on Manning's cellphone.

"It's summer school," he said. "It took me ten minutes while I was waiting for the bus."

"Smarty pants. You know you don't *have* to do what Grandpa says, right? Anytime you feel overloaded, you tell me, and I'll talk to him."

"I know, Mom." He sighed, hitting play on "House of the Rising Sun" before he started scrolling for the next song. When it came to electronics, he had the same attention span as our two-year-old. "I'm not worried about my classes, but . . . there is something else."

I took the phone from him, setting it aside. "What's the matter?" I asked.

He swung his legs under the table, watching Manning and Henry. He waited until they'd gone around the side of the shed to throw balls for the dogs.

Mateo turned to me. He had dark, wide-set eyes that sometimes seemed wise beyond his years—and other times, like now, he just looked like a shy kid. "There's a rumor going around school," he said.

"About?"

"Us."

My breath caught. I'd known this was coming, but I'd hoped I'd be more prepared. With the life Manning and I had led, there was plenty of gossip to choose from. Was it that Manning had fallen for a sixteen-year-old? Or the fact that he was an ex-con? Or that I'd stolen my sister's husband? Mateo didn't hide the fact that he was adopted—all his classmates knew—but only the principal and our family had the details of his situation.

I braced myself for whatever bombshell Manning and I had constructed for ourselves and brought on our children. "What's the rumor?"

"That Dad's a criminal."

Shit. My heart fell. Behind door number two—a mistake Manning and I had made in our youths that would haunt us forever. Though we'd gone on to live a fulfilling and rewarding life since then, I hated that decisions made long ago would affect not just us, but our kids. Knowing how sensitive Manning was about his record, and how protective he was of the family, he would *not* be happy to hear this.

Mateo and I were speaking quietly, but Manning came around the corner and instantly knew something was up. "What are you two talking about?"

We sat still and silent, as though we'd been busted. "Um," I said. "School."

"Yeah? What about it?" He pointed a screwdriver at Mateo. "You get a bad grade or what?"

"Not yet," Mateo said. "But I'm working on it."

Manning laughed. "Atta boy. So what's with the long faces?"

I checked on Henry, who was trying to get Mads and Cola to sit still to play Duck Duck Goose. I supposed, at some point, I'd become one of the adults around here, so I had to act like one. "Mateo heard something at school," I said, keeping my voice low. "About our past."

"Ah." Manning set the screwdriver down and crossed his arms. "What was it?"

"They say you went to jail," Mateo said. "But that's a lie. Your *dad* went to jail, not you."

Mateo knew the gritty details about Manning's sister's death. When he'd first come into our home, he'd acted tough but was as scared and confused as Manning and I had expected. Not only was there a lot of commotion and crying with the new baby, but Manning was an intimidating man, and Mateo had just defended his sister from being beaten to death by *killing* an intimidating man.

Manning had sat Mateo down and told him all about his past, the way Madison had drowned, how he'd almost gotten in trouble for it, and how he no longer communicated with his own parents. It had bonded them, and I'd come to realize this adoption hadn't only been about Mateo. Manning had also needed to feel like he'd truly helped. Bringing Mateo here meant Manning had finally ended a dark chapter in his life. A weight had been lifted.

Manning had shown Mateo many things since then, but most importantly, he'd taught him how to trust, how to confront his past to protect his future, and how a man treated the people he loved. As a new mom with a set of problems all my own, I would never forget how Manning had ensured Mateo understood the responsibility that came with having a newborn in the house.

Of course, we'd been saving the jail story for when Mateo was a little older, but it seemed as though some town gossips had decided that time would be now.

"So where'd you hear this rumor?" Manning asked.

"The kids at school."

"Which ones?"

It was an odd question that had me wrinkling my nose at Manning. "Why does it matter?"

Mads stepped on Cola's paw, and he yelped loudly enough that she started to cry. Manning turned, but I picked her up first so he could focus on Mateo.

"Which kids, Mat?" Manning asked.

"Well, a lot of them. Like my friends," Mateo said. "Michael said he heard from his mom, who heard it from the principal's secretary that . . ."

Manning wiped his hands on his jeans. "That what?"

Mateo lowered his voice. "You're so dangerous, you can kill a man with your bare hands."

"*What?*" I screeched, bouncing Mads as I whipped my head back and forth between Mateo and Manning. "Are they fucking kidding?"

"Lake, it's all right." Manning shook his head quickly before turning to Mateo. "I did go to jail. Prison, actually. There's a difference."

Mateo's brows drew together. "You told me you didn't."

"I never said that. I told you my dad went away for hurting Madison. Me, I was arrested many years later for a robbery I didn't commit."

"You were innocent?" Mateo stopped moving his feet, his knuckles whitening as he gripped the table. "That's . . . that's not *fair.*"

"Yeah, and it made me angry for a long time. Your mom, too. But that was twenty-something years ago. Look at the life we've built since then. Look at our family."

Mateo glanced at me and Mads. "Your dad and I have made mistakes," I said. "Some of them very serious. But we don't let them rule our lives or change the kind of people we are." I set Madison on the table next to Mateo, lightly holding her there. She reached a chubby hand up, smiling sunshine at him. "We treat people with kindness and respect, and we get that in return."

Mateo patted her on the head. I had no doubt he was thinking about his own sister, whom he hadn't seen since they'd been separated as kids.

Manning nodded at Mateo. "You asked me if it was wrong to defend your sister the way you did? If you're a bad kid?"

Mateo put his hand back on the table, blinking at the ground. "Yeah."

"You're not," Manning said. "You're a man, and a good one, aren't you?"

A good man. Chills rose over my skin. It was like watching Manning tell his younger self that there were great things in his future, and that he deserved them.

Mateo was pensive a moment. He was a smart kid, and we'd always treated his past with respect. We didn't want to cover it up or sugarcoat it or try to erase it. It hadn't always been the easiest route, but it meant we could have these conversations with him now. Mateo nodded. "I want to be."

"Don't let your past threaten what's ahead of you, Mat." Manning's already powerful gaze intensified as he met my eyes. "We all make mistakes, but it was your mom who taught me that only I could decide whether to move forward as a coward or as a man. It's up to you to make the same choice."

———

After lunch, we sat around the picnic table in the front yard with empty plates and full stomachs. Mateo played a game on Manning's phone while Henry watched, rapt. The dogs surrounded us, hoping for scraps, as Manning sat across the table from me with Madison in his lap.

"You can't leave that girl alone for five minutes, can you?" I asked. I'd been ready to put her down for a nap before lunch, but Manning had insisted I wait until he went back to work so he could spend time with her.

"Don't worry, Birdy." He reached across the table, holding his palm face up. "You're always number one in my eyes."

I waved him off but took his hand. He pulled my arm taut until I was forced to stand. "What do you want?" I asked with a laugh.

"Come over here."

I released his hand and switched from my side of the picnic table to his. "Better?" I asked.

"You have no idea."

I smoothed pesky frown lines from between his eyebrows. Was he still thinking about what Mateo had said? We hadn't been trying to hide Manning's history considering the crime had gone down in Big Bear, but I'd hoped enough time had passed that people wouldn't make the connection, or if they did, that they'd have the decency to keep it to themselves.

"I'm going to call the school in the morning," I said, checking to make sure the boys were still glued to the cellphone.

"What's the school going to do?"

"I don't know but it makes me *so* mad that someone would go around spreading rumors about us—"

"Not us," he said. "Me."

"I'll start with the principal's secretary—"

"Grace?"

"Yes, *Grace*. She's a relentless *gossip*."

"Yeah, she is."

"I mean, come *on*. You can *kill* a man with your bare hands?" I shook my head. "Ridiculous. Who would say such a thing?"

Manning kissed Maddy's cheek. "Someone who wants the whole town to know how dangerous I am, I guess. What do you think, Mads? Is Daddy scary?"

She smiled. "Daddy scary. Daddy kiss."

"You're not scary," I said. "Not even close."

Manning shifted Mads to his other side to put an arm around me. "Lake?"

"Yeah, Bear?"

"Don't call the school."

"Why not?"

"It's just a rumor. If people want to think I'm dangerous, let them."

I frowned. A lot of his early life, Manning had thought of himself as a bad person. It'd taken me years and a great deal of heartbreak to get him to see that wasn't true. I hoped Mateo's recent introspection didn't have Manning questioning his own past. "You're a *good* man," I told him.

"Yeah, but we don't need that getting out."

"What are you talking about?" I asked, drawing back to look at him.

He had his eyes on Madison, and they were filled with pure adoration. I realized then that he hadn't even finished his second sandwich. There were still a few bites on his plate, not to mention a small pile of chips. Only one person had ever held Manning's attention long enough that he'd forgotten to eat. Well, now there were two of us. *That* was the power this little girl had over him.

The kind of power that would make a man do crazy things.

But exactly *how* crazy?

I gasped, leaning back to point at him. "Manning Raymond Sutter."

"Lake Dolly Sutter."

"*You* started the rumor, didn't you?"

"Don't be ridiculous," he said, but the corner of his mouth twitched.

"You went to Grace and everything." I gaped at him. "But why?"

He shrugged, picking a chip off his plate to toss it in his mouth. "Why do you think, Mama Bear?" He

307

pressed his lips to the side of Madison's head, swaying with her. "Who's going to wander into these woods knowing there's a big, bad bear waiting?"

Our protector. Our great and apparently dangerous bear. My Manning. I didn't know what to say. "I can't believe you," I teased.

He shrugged. "I want to make sure people know."

"What people?"

He responded swiftly and without mercy. "Fucking *boys*."

I burst out laughing, even though hearing Manning curse in front of the kids was nearly enough to shock me into cardiac arrest. Even Mateo looked up from his game.

"She's *two*," I said.

"Have to start young. Do you see this little girl? She'll drive the world crazy with her mom's blue eyes."

It was true that Madison, a black-haired, blue-eyed Daddy's girl was bound to cause us some trouble. "Good thing she has you *and* two brothers."

"Plus a badass mom who can drive a stick," he said. He pulled me back against his side as I laughed. I had to admit, I enjoyed driving a manual now, and not only because it reminded me of the life-changing moment I'd found out I was pregnant with Henry.

I ran my hand up Manning's back, over the tattoo on his shoulder, which had grown by many stars. "You're something else, you know that?" I told him.

"You too, Birdy. Give me a kiss."

"Oh—hang on," I said, digging my hand into the back pocket of my jeans. "I've got something for you."

He lowered his mouth to my ear. "That right, Mrs. Sutter? What're you keeping in your pants for me?"

"Not that," I said, bumping him with my shoulder. I took out a tin of Candy Kisses lip balm I'd found in some old boxes my mom and dad had brought on their last visit. I smoothed it on as Manning watched, flicking his tongue over his bottom lip.

"That the good stuff?" he asked. "The one I've been asking about for *years*?"

"Watermelon." I leaned into him, looking up into his eyes. "Happy anniversary of the day we met twenty-five years ago."

"Happy anniversary, sweet girl. You know you make me the happiest man alive."

"Show me how happy. Kiss the watermelon right off my lips, Great Bear."

And he did.

TITLES BY
JESSICA HAWKINS
LEARN MORE AT JESSICAHAWKINS.NET

SLIP OF THE TONGUE
THE FIRST TASTE
YOURS TO BARE

SOMETHING IN THE WAY SERIES
SOMETHING IN THE WAY
SOMEBODY ELSE'S SKY
MOVE THE STARS
LAKE + MANNING

THE CITYSCAPE SERIES
COME UNDONE
COME ALIVE
COME TOGETHER

EXPLICITLY YOURS SERIES
POSSESSION
DOMINATION
PROVOCATION
OBSESSION

ABOUT THE AUTHOR

JESSICA HAWKINS is a *USA Today* bestselling author known for her "emotionally gripping" and "off-the-charts hot" romance. Dubbed "queen of angst" by both peers and readers for her smart and provocative work, she's garnered a cult-like following of fans who love to be torn apart...and put back together.

She writes romance both at home in California and around the world, a coffee shop traveler who bounces from café to café with just a laptop, headphones, and a coffee cup. She loves to keep in close touch with her readers, mostly via Facebook, Instagram, and her mailing list.

CONNECT WITH JESSICA

Stay updated & join the
JESSICA HAWKINS Mailing List
www.JESSICAHAWKINS.net/mailing-list

www.amazon.com/author/jessicahawkins
www.facebook.com/jessicahawkinsauthor
twitter: @jess_hawk

Made in United States
North Haven, CT
20 May 2022

19376823R00190